THE STRANGE GIFT OF GWENDOLYN GOLDEN

TO Ava,

enjoy the flight!

THE STRANGE GIFT OF GWENDOLYN GOLDEN

by

Philippa Dowding

Philippa Dowding

Toronto
2014

DUNDURN
TORONTO

Editor: Allister Thompson
Design: Courtney Horner
Printer: Webcom

Library and Archives Canada Cataloguing in Publication

Dowding, Philippa, 1963-, author

The strange gift of Gwendolyn Golden / by Philippa Dowding.

Issued in print and electronic formats.
ISBN 978-1-4597-0735-1

I. Title.

PS8607.O9874S77 2014   jC813'.6   C2013-902957-5
                                                 C2013-902958-3

1   2   3   4   5   18   17   16   15   14

  Conseil des Arts   Canada Council   Canada    ONTARIO ARTS COUNCIL
         du Canada   for the Arts   CONSEIL DES ARTS DE L'ONTARIO

We acknowledge the support of the Canada Council for the Arts which last year invested $20.1 million in writing and publishing throughout Canada. Nous remercions de son soutien le Conseil des Arts du Canada, qui a investi 20,1 millions de dollars l'an dernier dans les lettres et l'édition à travers le Canada.

We acknowledge the support of the **Canada Council for the Arts** and the **Ontario Arts Council** for our publishing program. We also acknowledge the financial support of the **Government of Canada** through the **Canada Book Fund** and **Livres Canada Books**, and the **Government of Ontario** through the **Ontario Book Publishing Tax Credit** and the **Ontario Media Development Corporation**.

Care has been taken to trace the ownership of copyright material used in this book. The author and the publisher welcome any information enabling them to rectify any references or credits in subsequent editions.

                                                            J. Kirk Howard, President

Permission for use of Gwendolyn MacEwen's poem, "Fragments from a Childhood," was provided by the author's family.

VISIT US AT
Dundurn.com | Definingcanada.ca | @dundurnpress | Facebook.com/dundurnpress

Dundurn   Gazelle Book Services Limited   Dundurn
3 Church Street, Suite 500   White Cross Mills   2250 Military Road
Toronto, Ontario, Canada   High Town, Lancaster, England   Tonawanda, NY
M5E 1M2   LA1 4XS   U.S.A. 14150

For Sarah,
my amazing flying girl

"Something has come to pass, you think,
something more important than
a mere flight over the ravine."
— Gwendolyn MacEwen,
"Fragments from a Childhood"

ONE

This morning I wake up on the ceiling.

Which is odd, because I've never woken up there before, not that I remember, anyway. I'm pretty sure I would remember something like that. It's not exactly the kind of thing that happens every day.

At least, not to me.

I wake up, and for a moment I can't figure out where I am. My carpet is on the ceiling. I can't understand why I am looking up at my bed, or why Cassie, my fat brown and white beagle, is also sitting on the ceiling.

My arms are floating out at my sides, too, and my long brown hair is dangling, well, up.

That's when I start to wake up and figure it out.

I'm up. Too far up. Up on the ceiling, in fact. And everything that is generally on the ground (like the carpet and my dog), is too far down. I'm not sure what to do. I try pointing my toes toward the carpet, but nothing happens. My feet just rise again and rest softly on the ceiling behind me.

I slowly circle the room, making swimming motions with my arms. Cassie circles around beneath me, worried, looking up, whining and wagging her tail. That's when I hear someone walking along the hallway toward my room.

My mom knocks on the door. "Gwennie! Are you up?" she calls.

"Yes! Yes, Mom, I'm up! Don't come in!" I call back.

I certainly am up. Way up. I get a little panicky. I do *not* want my mom to come into the room and find me stuck to the ceiling, like a little kid's party balloon. I can't begin to imagine the freak-out that will cause. I have to do something.

I air-swim gently along the ceiling in my pink nightie until I bump into the top of the bedpost, which I grab with both hands. As soon as I touch it, I fall like a rock and smack hard onto the floor.

My mom opens the door. I'm sitting beside the bed, rubbing my behind, which took quite a beating when I fell.

"Gwennie, are you okay?" She looks concerned.

"Yeah. Yeah, Mom, I just fell out of bed. I'm fine."

She looks a little worried but seems convinced. "Okay, hurry up and get ready for school." She leaves and shuts the door.

Cassie comes over and licks my face. My dog is the only one who knows what a liar I am.

This is an interesting start to the day. A troubling and unusual start, but definitely interesting.

You might think that I'd be disturbed at waking up on the ceiling of my room. You'd be right. I really *should* feel disturbed and perhaps a little worried about my sanity, but honestly, I can't say that I am. A lot of weird things have been going on with me lately. Mostly puberty, I guess. I mean, growing three inches in three months, getting your period, and growing boobs isn't exactly normal. Well, everyone says it is, but it doesn't feel so normal.

So what's a little early-morning floating around your room compared to that?

It happened. I wasn't dreaming. I woke up on the ceiling.

So what *am* I feeling?

Nothing. Just more of the same nothing, I guess.

TWO

I wash my face, brush my teeth, and get dressed. I go down to the kitchen. My little brother and sister are arguing over the breakfast cereal, which I grab then pour them both a bowl.

"Can't you two share anything? It's not that hard," I say.

"He's always grabbing stuff!" Christine says. "It's rude."

"She always wants everything first. It's annoying," Christopher says at the same time.

Yes, you heard me. Unfortunately, their names are Christine and Christopher. They're twins. I begged my mother *not* to name them the same thing. What were we going to call them for short? I'd asked her. How would they feel about having practically the same name? And wouldn't they hate their names? Wouldn't they each think their name was really meant for the opposite sex? Christine would think her name was a boy's name, and Christopher would think his name was meant for girls.

It was a bad idea all around, but it didn't seem to bother my mother. Since Dad wasn't around when they were born, I didn't have anyone else to try to talk sense into her. Sometimes when I talk to them both at the same time, I call them C2 if I'm feeling nice, or the Chrissies if I'm not because they both hate the name Chrissie. It makes them cry.

My mother deserves that, she really does.

I eat my toast and jam, sneak a cup of really strong coffee, which I'm not supposed to have, and get the twins' lunch ready.

Mom drops us off at Bass Creek Junior School, and I walk the Chrissies to the front door, but they walk themselves to class. They're pretty self-sufficient, having each other to rely on and everything.

I walk to my school next door, Bass Creek Senior School, for the grade sevens and eights: the schizophrenic years. Us grade eights share lunch-time with the little kids from the junior school, but we have gym with the giant grade nine girls from the high school down the street. It's like no one can decide if we're children or teenagers.

The town planners weren't very imaginative, either, since our high school, our public schools, and our town all have the same name: Bass Creek.

Which is odd, because there isn't a creek, a stream, or a puddle anywhere near town. There's one of the great lakes, though, an hour to the south. Mom says there was a creek once, a long time ago, before the highway was built and all the local rivers and streams (and creeks presumably) were diverted or buried. It always seemed unfair to me, forcing water to do something other than it wants to, but I'm not in charge here.

My first class is English, a class I'm never too crazy about. I'm not much of a reader. Our teacher, Mr. Marcus, wants us to write a half-hour, in-class essay that starts with the three words, "If I could...."

If I could ... what? What am I supposed to write? Mr. Marcus is in love with making us write these scenarios where we're supposed to imagine ourselves differently.

Differently enough to wake up floating on the ceiling, I wonder?

So I write: "If I could, I'd name Christine and Christopher something better, like Isabelle and Rodolphus. Or Cynthia and Michael. Or Emma and Shiloh. Nothing rhyming, nothing with the same sequence of letters, nothing embarrassing and stupid...."

That's as far as I get, because that's when my foot starts to float off the floor.

I accidentally boot Jeffrey Parks, the boy sitting facing me, in the shin. It isn't my fault. My foot just starts floating slowly, and suddenly my running shoe is jammed into his leg.

"Ouch! What the heck, Gwen? What are you doing?" Jeffrey's eyes get squinty and scared, and he moves away from me really quick.

Now, Jeffrey Parks and I have had words before. We aren't exactly the best of friends. He once teased me about the wrong thing in grade five (I'd recently had a *very bad* haircut), and I punched him so hard he cried every time he saw me for days afterwards.

But really, today, this particular incident is nothing personal. I have no control over myself, this time. My eyes get really wide. I *am not* going to float up to the ceiling in the middle of my grade eight English class. It just isn't going to happen.

I jump up so fast that my desk falls over. My pencils and papers go flying, which is just as well, because it distracts everyone. They're all running around trying to pick up my stuff. I run toward the door, and all I can say to Mr. Marcus as I run by is, "Sorry, sir, I think I'm going to throw up!"

That's the kids' "get out of jail free" pass. No teacher is going to make you stay and talk if they think you are about to barf your breakfast all over their shoes.

He just nods and opens the door extra wide for me. I leave that room *really* fast, believe me. So fast, that no one notices that as I run away, my feet aren't actually touching the ground.

THREE

I run down that hallway as fast as I can and burst into the staff supply room, the nearest room I can find with a lock on the door. It's really odd, running without touching the ground. It feels a little like when you try to run in those bouncy inflatable castles you find at rich kids' birthday parties, or at the town fair.

I slam the door and lock it behind me. Technically, I'm not supposed to be in the staff supply room, but this is an emergency. Gail Todd came in here last year when she had her period and didn't want everyone to know. I figure this is at least as serious as that.

I hold on to the door handle, not sure what to do. I'm breathing fast and my heart is pounding. To make matters worse, my feet gently start to float toward the ceiling. I don't want to let go of the handle for anything, so I float horizontally for a while, then as my feet rise toward the ceiling, I'm head down with my toes pointing skyward. It isn't very comfortable. As the blood rushes to my head, I start to feel dizzy, so I have to let go of the door handle.

As soon as my body is free, it floats lazily toward the ceiling, where it bounces around for a few moments, then settles gently, bumping up and down against the ceiling tiles.

I realize that I'm now talking about my body like an "it," like it's no longer connected to the rest of me. But that's what it feels like. As if my body is totally in charge, and I'm just going along for the ride.

Which I guess I am.

I edge away from the hot light fixture on the ceiling. No sense getting third degree burns all over me. I look around.

The supply room is where the teachers get their extra pencils and paper and their classroom supplies for arts and crafts. It's filled with shelves of coloured paper and huge, econo-sized buckets of non-toxic paint. It's also filled with strange classroom leftovers, like giant papier-mâché puppets that were too good to throw away, but not good enough to display in the school foyer.

This is why, as I float around on the ceiling, I come face-to-face with a huge clown puppet that the grade nines made for a play last year. The clown was creepy then. It's even creepier now, looming out at me, grinning in the dark. A red nose, pointed eyebrows, and huge red mouth grin as I spin by in the air current.

"What's so funny?" I demand as I float by, but I suddenly worry that the clown is going to giggle and answer me in clown-rhyme: *"TEE HEE HEE! You're a freak, Gwendolyn Golden, just like MEEEE!"*

That would likely finish me off for good.

After that, I just try to avoid the stupid clown.

I float for about half an hour. I'm beginning to wonder if I will slowly deflate, like a helium balloon, before I can touch down again. It took my little brother's Batman balloon almost three days to deflate and sink to the ground last Halloween.

I can't wait three days. I'm starting to get a little panicky. What am I going to do?

Finally there's a knock on the door and I hear our principal, Mrs. Abernathy, calling through the crack.

"Hello? Are you in there, Gwendolyn?" Mrs. Abernathy says.

She sounds very sympathetic and nice. I've always liked her. She's really good in a crisis. Once she had to take Christopher to the hospital when he needed stitches in kindergarten, and my mom had to meet them there. But this isn't exactly a case of stitches. A crisis, perhaps, but probably not one that can be fixed with a quick visit to the hospital. Although that would be nice.

"Uh, yes! It's me in here," I say. I hope she doesn't notice that my voice is coming from the ceiling.

"Oh, is everything all right, dear?"

I can sense the worry in her voice. I reach out to steady myself, and as soon as I touch the door, I crash to the ground. It must have been loud, because I hear her gasp.

She rattles the doorknob. "Gwendolyn! Gwen! Are you okay?" she calls.

I stand up, brush off my shirt and jeans, straighten my long hair, and open the door.

Mrs. Abernathy and Mr. Marcus are both standing there.

"Are you okay, Gwen? We've been looking for you everywhere," Mr. Marcus says. He really sounds worried.

"Yeah, I think I'm fine now. I should go home, though."

The truth is that I feel fantastic. I try to look like I have been throwing up (but I don't have to lie because no one asks me if I did or didn't), but I actually feel incredible, better than I have in ages.

I can't explain it, but floating around on the ceiling seems to agree with me.

FOUR

I get my backpack and sign out at the office. I call my mom to come and get me, but she can't because she's in a meeting.

I have to walk home. Which poses an interesting problem.

What am I going to do if I start floating *outside*? In my bedroom, and in the staff supply room, there was a ceiling to keep me from floating off into space. What am I going to do if I start to lift off on Main Street, or in the park, or on the driveway, or in the millions of other places that I could use as a launching pad? Will I float along just off the ground or will I keep going, like a lost weather balloon, higher and higher and higher until I freeze, or pop?

For the first time, I start to feel truly scared.

I'm too young to float away into space. My family will miss me. I have to graduate from middle school in a few weeks. I want to go to high school! I want to learn to drive a car, and kiss somebody other than my mom, and watch a high school football game and cheer for a boy I secretly have a crush on.

It starts to rain and I stand outside the school under the front door overhang pondering the problem. There is no one around, so I decide to do a little test. I'll take a quick jog out into the rain and back under the overhang to see if I have any floating tendencies.

So I dash out into the raindrops, dance around a little, then run back to safety. My feet are very much planted on the ground. They are so planted on the ground that my shoes are wet and my socks are soaked through.

Okay, so no floating so far.

I do it again a few more times, dashing into the rain and out from the safety of the overhang, a little farther each time. Nothing happens. So I decide it's safe to try walking home.

As an added precaution, I find a large rock, which I put in my backpack. It's pretty heavy. I'm not sure if it will help to weigh me down if I start floating again, but I figure it can't hurt.

I step out from the overhang just as it starts to pour. I take the main street and the park and walk close to buildings and trees in case I have to grab on to anything to keep me from floating away.

But it's raining so hard that there isn't any chance of anything floating away in the downpour. Even birds hide in the trees. I scurry along the deserted main street, past the library and the local candy store, although the rock in my backpack does slow me down a little. I run across the park, keeping close to things to grab on to, but there isn't any reason to. I don't float.

I just get really soaked. When I finally run into my house and slam the door behind me, a huge puddle forms at my feet in about ten seconds. Water drips off me hard. I walk to the top of the laundry room stairs and peel off my wet clothes, which land with a heavy slosh on the floor. Cassie waddles into the front hall, wagging her tail.

"Hi, Cass, don't ask me to take you out for a walk, because I'm not going out in *that* again!"

After a hot shower I get into dry pyjamas and spend the rest of the afternoon curled up on the couch with Cassie, watching kiddie cartoons. Mom and the Chrissies come home around six o'clock after the twins' piano lesson, and we have a boring night doing homework and getting dinner and arguing about what to watch on TV. I almost forget about floating.

Until the next morning, when I wake up on the ceiling again.

FIVE

This time, I wake up with my feet dangling down toward the carpet as my body slowly circles the room. Cassie is sitting underneath me, quietly watchful. She doesn't seem as freaked out as she did yesterday. Which is good, I guess.

I must have been up here a long time. My head is lolling to one side and a little drool is sliding down my cheek, which I wipe off with my sleeve. It's odd, but floating is actually kind of a comfortable way to sleep. There aren't any tired spots on my body, nothing that fell asleep from lying on it. I stretch a little and wiggle my toes, which makes me look like I'm running in mid-air. I actually start to move around the room a little. So I try again. I move my legs like I'm on a bicycle, and I make a little progress in a straight line across the room. Like I'm walking.

Interesting. Circling my arms around like I'm swimming doesn't really work very well. But taking a few air-steps works.

Noted. I air-walk a few times around the room,

almost getting the hang of it. I'm still a little unsteady, and I don't always go exactly in the direction I want, but it's better. Just then, I hear my mom coming up the hallway stairs. I have to get down, fast!

Yesterday I fell to the floor like a rock when I touched the bedpost. This time I'll be more careful. I put both hands out and get ready to hold on tight. I touch the bedpost and nothing happens.

Uh-oh.

So it worked yesterday, but it isn't going to work today? How am I going to get down off the ceiling? I try forcing my way down the bedpost and get stuck halfway ... when Mom walks into the room. I look like a monkey, like a little kid climbing up and down the bedpost. I used to do that a lot when I was little, so I pretend I'm doing that now.

"Hi, Mom!" I say, as I hang on with one arm, my legs clamped around the bedpost for all I'm worth. Then I tickle under my other arm like a monkey. "OOH-OOH. Got any bananas?" I ask innocently. My heart is pounding in my chest, though, so don't think I'm not scared.

She looks at me like I'm crazy, then laughs. "You don't need any more bananas, Gwen! I think you *are* bananas!" she says, but comes over to ruffle my hair. As soon as she touches me, I can feel the weight re-enter my body, and my feet slowly slide down the bedpost to the floor. Touchdown. Phew. Feet firmly on the floor once again, I hug my mother.

She hugs me back, surprised. It seems like our first hug in ages.

SIX

I walk to school. Mom drives the twins, but I really feel like walking by myself, so she lets me. It's Friday morning and a beautiful spring day. All the rain from yesterday makes everything smell great, and the trees are starting to turn green. The grass is greener too, and flowers are coming up fast, those first ones, the little ones that look like bells, and the tall yellow ones.

I feel like skipping, I really do, just like a little kid. But I don't skip. I make myself walk along in the one-foot-in-front-of-the-other regular way. It's a struggle not to skip, but I'm kind of worried that skipping might lead to bouncing, which might give my body ideas about being weightless. And floaty.

That I don't need. I walk, but I keep a close eye on nearby trees and fences in case I have to grab on to anything to keep me earthbound.

But nothing remotely floaty happens.

So I walk. And as I walk, I bump into old Mr. McGillies, wearing his filthy long coat over his raggedy clothes. I've never seen him wear anything else, and I've known him my whole life. He's pushing a cart along, which is rattling because it's filled with empty bottles. Mr. McGillies grew up when milkmen dropped full bottles of milk off at your front door every morning, then collected the empty bottles every night. Now that he's old, people think he's pretending to be a milkman with all those empty bottles. But I think he just likes bottles. Some bottles he collects, and some he returns to the recycling depot for nickels. People think he's crazy, but Mom says he's just old, not crazy. I've always kind of liked him.

"Hi, Mr. McGillies. How are you today?"

He stops and looks up at me (he's really short). He pushes his thick glasses up his nose.

"Well, young Gwen. How's flyin'?" he says. I blink. Flyin'?

"Er. Flying?" I say, not altogether very intelligently. What does he mean? He can't possibly mean … *flying*, can he?

He cackles. He has a really funny laugh that always makes me laugh, too. He sounds a little like Grover from *Sesame Street* when he laughs. I smile. I can't help it. I've watched Mr. McGillies push his empty bottle cart around our neighbourhood since I was a little girl. He did always make me smile. But this is a bit odd — he's never mentioned flying before.

"Flying, Mr. McGillies? What do you mean?" I repeat.

He winks at me then and says, "Flying, missy. You heard me! You know exactly what I mean!" He cackles again, but this time I don't smile. I think my face must do a downturn, and I go from looking like I am being nice to Mr. McGillies to being horrified by him.

He starts to hum a little tune. "Scrub and wash, scrub and wash, scrub and wash the bottles," as he turns away. He's not getting off that easily.

I run up to him and stand in front of his bottle cart. I put my hand on the cart and ask him again, sterner this time, "What do you *mean*? Flying? What do you mean?" It's starting to dawn on me that Mr. McGillies knows something I don't. But he isn't owning up to anything. He cackles again.

"Oh no, Miss Gwennie. All in good time! All in good time! Don't fly away now!"

His old brown face splits into a wide smile, one of the widest smiles I've ever seen. How did I not notice that Mr. McGillies has a gold back tooth? I guess I've never seen him smile that wide before.

Then he trundles his cart away, and no matter how much I pester and yell and downright whine at him, he pretends he can't hear me and goes on humming his crazy man scrub-and-wash-the-bottles song. He shuffles off down the sidewalk.

Okay, this is just very odd. I shake my head and decide that despite what my mother thinks, maybe he *is* just a crazy old guy. A crazy old guy who somehow knows exactly what is happening to me.

I am going to have another chat with Mr. McGillies, really soon, but right now I have to get to school.

SEVEN

I make it through the morning at school without any body parts floating away from me.

It is actually such a dull morning that I catch myself wishing for that floating feeling.

It would be a welcome distraction from the boring lesson about local taxes in our Civics class. I've been taking Civics for almost seven months, and I still can't quite figure out what it's about. Sometimes we talk about helping old people and volunteering for things, and sometimes we talk about garbage collection. Those things I can pretty much understand as something that we all need to get behind, at least some of the time. But then our teacher goes on about salt or taxes, and I swear my body just goes limp. I simply cannot get my mind around what on earth she is talking about.

I wonder if there is some way I can pretend I need to throw up again, like yesterday? Or maybe get some mystery "cramping," which might get me a free hall pass to the nurse's office. It wouldn't work with this teacher, though, she's too smart for that — besides, she's a girl. That old "cramps" trick only works with guy teachers. Mr. Marcus always goes pale, for instance.

I sigh and wiggle in my seat. This simply has to stop. I am going to freak out if I have to listen to one more word about municipal taxes. What are they for, anyway? Who gets to decide how much tax we pay? I have a paper route on Saturdays, do I have to pay taxes? My head is starting to ache. I cheer up for a moment — maybe I *am* going to throw up.

Nope. False alarm. Okay, then.

I try to will my body to float. I try lifting my foot off the floor, but it just falls like a dead weight back to the tile beneath my desk. I lift the other one. Nothing. My running shoe makes a loud slapping sound as it hits down. "Sorry," I mumble as my teacher shoots me a warning look, which sadly doesn't stop her from babbling on about garbage taxes.

I slowly float my arm out to my side, but it's just as heavy as my leg. I try my other arm. Nothing. I've never felt so leaden and earthbound in my life.

At this point, I'd be happy with a floating finger. I try raising my index finger off the table. It almost hovers for a second, but no, I realize I'm holding it there.

Clearly I'm not going to float anywhere during Civics class, just when I really want to.

Noted. The *ability* to float seems to have nothing to do with the *desire* to float. In fact, it seems the more I want to float, the less likely it is that I will.

At this moment, in this class, I have as much chance of floating as a lead balloon.

EIGHT

There is nothing leaden about lunch, though. Oh no! That's all fun and games and up in the air time. Honestly, I'm starting to feel like a hot air balloon, with all this upping and downing. And I'm starting to want some answers. The novelty is definitely wearing off.

I guess I should back up a little. I'm having lunch with Jez. She's the best friend I've always had, since before we started school, I think before we could even speak. Our mothers met in the park when we were still too little to do anything but lie around in our strollers. Our mothers are actually nothing alike, so they must have been pretty desperate to meet up and become friends.

Jez's mom is about fifteen years younger than mine. Jez is short for Jezebel, which is a not-so-nice woman from the Bible, but Jez's mother didn't know that. She just liked the name. It *is* a pretty name, I think so too.

Anyway, at lunch Jez and I are sitting at a table eating french fries and dipping them in too much ketchup, which is how we like them. Martin Evells walks by us, and my stomach flips.

Okay, so what? I like Martin. I always have. It's not really my fault. He's nice and he smells like lemons. We were best friends the year we were six.

"Hi, Gwen," he says then walks away.

My stomach does its flippy thing, then under the table my foot leaves the floor. Just for a second. Which wouldn't have been such a problem if it didn't kick Jez on its journey.

"Ouch. Gwen. What was that for? Martin always says hi to you." Jez looks really hurt. She's gripping her calf where I booted her.

Uh-oh. I'm definitely starting to feel something. A kind of tingling and burning up and down my arms and legs. I grab her by the wrist and I swear I yank that girl out of her chair. I start sashaying across the lunchroom and out the door, dragging my best friend behind me.

She doesn't go willingly. She fights me all the way. Luckily the lunchroom at our school is really noisy (since it's got the junior *and* senior kids in it), so no one pays much attention to me dragging my unwilling friend out the door.

"Ow! Gwennie, stop it. What are you doing? I wasn't finished my lunch! I'm still hungry!" She gets all weird and whiney. I don't have time for weird and whiney. That feeling, that weightless feeling, is starting to take over. I'm tingling like I'm on fire, and I know what's coming.

I run us down the empty school hallway into the girl's washroom and push us into the big wheelchair stall at the end. I slam the bolt behind me then spin around and look at her. I must look a little scary, because she backs away from me until she bumps into the bathroom door. Her eyes get really big and her mouth falls open.

Yep. She's scared. I know that look.

"Okay, Jez. You can't get that look on your face or I'm going to lose it. Just calm down. Okay? Jez? Just shut your eyes for a minute, and I'll explain."

Jez shut her eyes really tight and nods. "Uh-huh," she manages to say, but she still keeps her eyes shut. "What's going on, Gwennie?" She sounds really scared now. Poor Jez.

I slowly start to float up to the ceiling. There's nothing I can do. I'm gone, floating, spinning slowly above the stall, looking straight down onto the top of my best friend's head. I sigh.

There's no easy way to do this. I just have to tell her.

"Okay, Jez. You can open your eyes when I say, but you have to promise not to scream. Actually, you have to promise not to make any noise at all. Okay? Just don't do anything? Just look?"

She nods and I say, "Okay, you can open them."

Jez starts breathing funny and jagged, but she bravely nods, and with a little whimper, she opens her eyes. She slowly looks up, first at my dangling feet, then at my legs, then at my body and finally up into my face. It's in slow motion, just like in a horror movie, when the camera moves slowly up to the horrifying thing hanging from the ceiling.

That horrifying thing is me.

Jez stops breathing and just stares at me. Her eyes are gigantic, like mini soccer balls, and she slowly moves her hands up to her mouth. But she doesn't scream.

I really love Jez at this moment.

"Thank you for not screaming," I say. I also want to say, "Don't cry, Jez," because in the next second, two giant tears slide down my best friend's cheeks.

I don't cry, though. For one thing, since I'm hovering right over Jez's head, my tears will fall on her and soak her (it's a bit gross, the thought of crying on someone).

But for another thing, I can't cry.

I haven't cried in a long time. It's been so long, I can't remember the last time. So long, I think I might have forgotten how.

NINE

Jez just stands there, covering her mouth and looking up at me with her gigantic brown eyes.

I say again, "Jez, please stop crying." She nods really hard, which is what she always does when she wants to do what you ask but doesn't know how. She gulps.

"Stop nodding, too," I add. She nods really hard then suddenly stops. I can see her trying to pull herself together. She draws a deep breath, pulls some toilet paper off the roll, and dries her eyes.

"Okay. Okay. I'm not crying. I'm not," she whispers. I'm not sure why she is whispering, since there isn't anyone else in the bathroom. She looks up at me. She looks so sad and scared, I really want to hug her, but it's out of the question since I am up on the ceiling and all.

"Gwen, what are you doing up there?" She is still whispering. "Can't you get down?"

"I can't explain what I'm doing up here. It's been happening since yesterday. And I'm not sure how to get down. Sometimes I come down when I touch things, but it doesn't always work," I say doubtfully. I really don't want to fall to the ground again. This is an old school, built eighty years ago or something, when high ceilings were all the rage. At the moment, I'm floating way above the floor. I really don't want to fall from this height. I've already got a few giant bruises from yesterday.

"Okay, well go over to the wall above the window, that way if you come down, you can land in the sink and not fall too far," Jez says, wringing her hands a little. She's always brave, but I'm proud of her for handling this so well.

"Good idea." I slowly force my legs down to the floor and start air-walking toward the window. Jez follows underneath me, looking up, still wringing her hands. I hover above the sink, and I'm just about to put out my hand, when the bathroom door opens.

Shelley Norman, a big grade nine girl, walks in. Jez shrieks. I whip my hand out and touch the window, saying a little prayer: *this better work*.

It does. Next thing I know, I'm lying on Shelley Norman. I fall like a stone and land on this beefy grade nine girl. At least she breaks my fall. She shoves me off her and glowers at me. She's mean. She's breathing mean and nasty all over Jez and me.

"What the heck are you doing, Golden? Didn't I tell you in gym class last week never to touch me? Geez, you're crazier than everyone thinks," Shelley says. She looks like she is going to turn me into stone.

"She's not feeling well, Shelley," Jez says. "We're just going to the principal's office."

Jez grabs me and we tear out of there as fast as we can. I can actually feel Shelley Norman's mean, hot breath on my neck as we squeeze by her.

As we run down the corridor I sneak a quick peek at my best friend, who for the first time in our lives looks back at me like she has no idea who I am.

TEN

After Jez and I run out of the bathroom, I can tell she is really upset, because she's clutching my arm, like she does in scary movies when she's about to start screaming. Unfortunately, this isn't a movie, although I'm starting to wish it was. I really don't want my best friend to start screaming, though, because then I will be kind of convinced that I *am* a freak.

I'm pretty convinced already.

We make our way outside to the sidewalk in front of the school and start walking back and forth. I eye some trees nearby in case I start to float away and need to grab on to something quick.

Jez doesn't say anything for a few minutes, then she blurts out, "Okay, Gwennie Golden, what's going on? You ... you were ... you can *fly!*" I have to hush her up; even people far away are looking over at her, because she's shouting.

"Shhh, Jez. Quiet, I don't need people hearing us."

Just then Christopher and Christine come running up. I must look pretty weird or freaked out, because my little sister says, "What's wrong with *you*? You ran into the bathroom at lunchtime." At the same time my little brother says, "You were supposed to help us get french fries."

Shoot. I forgot about that. I *did* promise my mother that I'd help the twins buy themselves french fries at lunch today. Now they're getting older, she wants them to start to learn the basics of how to survive on the planet, starting with the essentials, like how to purchase french fries in a busy school cafeteria lineup.

"Sorry, guys, I kind of had an emergency. I forgot. We'll do it on Monday, okay?" The twins eye me curiously. Sometimes it seems like they are using both their brains as one big brain and secretly working things out between themselves, without talking. I swear they are brain-talking together about me now as they look at me.

"Yeah, Gwen had an emergency ...," my little brother says.

"... because she had to go poop!" my little sister says. Then the two of them run off together, laughing hysterically.

"They're weird," Jez says, watching them go. I must look hurt, because she says quickly, "Sorry, but they are. I swear they think together before they speak."

"Yeah, sometimes it seems like that. Look, lunch is almost over. I don't know what's going on. I woke up yesterday morning on the ceiling. It happened this morning, too. I don't know why."

"Well, are you feeling okay, otherwise?" she asks. Jez is a born mother — that's all she ever asks anyone, if they're feeling okay.

"Yeah." I nod. "That's the really weird part. I actually feel fantastic. I mean, I feel really, really great. I wake up on the ceiling, and it's like the best sleep I've ever had in my life."

"But how do you get up there?"

"How the heck do I know? I just wake up there. It's been happening here at school, though, which is weirder."

Jez actually laughs. "Weirder? What could be weirder than waking up on your ceiling, Gwen? Does your mom know?" As soon as she says it, she realizes how that sounds.

She shakes her head. "No, of course she doesn't know, does she?"

I shrug. "What do you think? I'm not going to tell her I've been flying around my room at night. She's already got enough to deal with."

I bite my lip and look away. We don't talk about that, Jez and I.

About what my mother has to deal with.

ELEVEN

Okay, so I know you're going to make a big deal about that last sentence, and you shouldn't. You really shouldn't. But I know you'll be thinking about it, so I'm just going to deal with it now, and then it'll be over.

My dad died seven years, one month, and eleven days ago, right before the twins were born. He was out one night during a freak storm, where things like cows and trees went missing. He went out to check on a neighbour, then we never saw him again.

We have a box with his stuff in it, stuff Mom calls "mementos," but I don't know what that is exactly since I've never seen inside. I've never even seen the box. It's in her closet and she never brings it out.

Ever.

We never found his body, either.

We had a funeral.

The casket was empty.

Now you know.

TWELVE

Jez and I have gym class after lunch.

We share the class with the grade nine girls, which is quite awful, especially if we are playing dodgeball or something. They are so much bigger than us, and better shots. Unfortunately, our gym teacher, Mr. Short (who is actually very tall), really loves dodgeball. And he has this unnatural belief that every teenager loves dodgeball, too.

Who wouldn't love being pelted with heavy rubber balls?

We walk into the gym in our shorts and sneakers. Yep. We're playing dodgeball. Shelley Norman bangs into me with her shoulder and snickers.

"Get ready to pay, Golden."

I'm in for it. I might as well paint a target on myself right now. Sure enough, every shot from Shelley is directed right at me. I get pretty banged up. I get a shot right in the head, but Mr. Short has his back turned and doesn't notice.

Jez tries to protect me for a while, but Shelley is

a wicked shot and keeps missing Jez and hitting me. I'm a magnet. Shelley can't miss.

Eventually I just give up. Balls are bouncing off me in all directions. The other grade nine girls start to join in and the pack mentality really takes over.

I start to feel sad. But I start to feel a little angry, too. And with that little feeling of anger, I also get a tiny tingling in my foot. Then both my feet. My arm starts to float out to my side. Even though I don't want to, I start yelling, "What's wrong with you, Shelley Norman? Can't you just leave me alone?!"

The grade nine girls back up a little. Balls bounce slowly to stillness and the class gets quiet. The girls know what's coming. They've all seen my bad temper leak out before, and they're smart enough to be wary. One of them even says, "It's okay, Gwen, just calm down. We were just kidding around...."

But it's too late. I'm yelling at the top of my lungs and I can't turn it off. It's like a light switch got stuck on. Mr. Short finally starts to pay attention and blows his whistle, and Jez takes the opportunity to start running me out of the gym and down the school hallway. She has her arms locked around my shoulders as we run. I'm yelling my head off, and scared students are jumping out of our way.

I must look pretty crazy. Crazier than normal.

Jez runs with me into the staff washroom, clinging onto me like a vice. I've never noticed how strong she is in the arms. As soon as she slams the door behind us and locks it, she lets me go. I bob gently up to the ceiling, all the fight gone out of me.

I stop yelling and just float there, swirling around in the current like a lost balloon. Jez reaches up and grabs my shoelace then gently tugs me back down to Earth. I float slowly toward her, and she looks exactly like a little kid pulling a balloon down from the ceiling on a string.

When I bob eye-to-eye in front of her, she puts her arms around me and I whisper, "Don't let me go, Jez. Just don't let me go."

"I won't," she whispers back. "I promise."

THIRTEEN

But after a while, Jez's arms get tired and she has to let me go. I bob back up to the ceiling.

It takes about half an hour for me to stop floating, so Jez and I just stay in the staff washroom chatting. It gets kind of normal having my best friend sitting on the floor of the teachers' washroom with me up on the ceiling, talking about old times. It's sort of like when you're sick and miss a lot of school, and your friend comes over when you're getting better, to talk and bring you back into the world.

We both notice that no one ever seems to use the staff washroom, because no one comes knocking. We also notice it's a lot cleaner than the girls' bathroom. We hear people walking around in the hallway outside, but no one seems to be looking for me. Maybe after yesterday's experience in English, the teachers have decided to leave me alone if I start acting all crazy. Maybe they think it might be better that way, since no one wants to deal with crazy Gwennie Golden when she's having one of her screaming fits.

No one except Jez.

I float around for a bit, then as we laugh and talk and Jez gets kind of used to me up on the ceiling, I slowly float back down to Earth.

After that little episode in gym class, though, I notice people avoid me more than usual. All afternoon, kids dart little glances at me, then look away. They all think I have anger issues, anyway. I'm not exactly the most level-headed kid in the school at the best of times. Now and then I do blow up at someone for no real reason. So even without me flying around the room, people usually say things like "It's about her dad" when they're talking about me.

But they're way off on that.

It's not about him.

It's really about the fact that I'm flying around and I don't know how to stop. That's really what's going on here.

When I am firmly on the ground again, Jez and I leave the washroom and go back to the principal's office. We have to sign ourselves back into our next class, which is math. As we are getting our late slips, Mrs. Abernathy comes out of her office and calls to us. We walk over to her and she says, "Gwendolyn, Jez, I hear there was some excitement in gym class."

That's what she always calls trouble, "excitement." We both look at her. If only she knew how truly exciting it was, or could have been if I'd broken free of Jez's vice grip and floated to the ceiling of the gym in front of everyone.

I have a sudden image of myself bobbing against the light fixtures, way up on the gym ceiling, with all the kids down below me, laughing and pointing. The custodians would have to get the big outdoor ladder, the one they use to get soccer balls off the roof, to try to get me down. Maybe that wouldn't be big enough, though, and they'd have to get the lifesaving extendable hooks from the pool to try to grapple me back down.

I suddenly imagine the school custodian and his assistant lassoing my arms and legs with ropes. They'd say useful things like, "Easy with her now, don't let her head bounce too much." Or, "Watch her legs don't hit the window, we don't want to break it." And other helpful things like that.

And maybe even that wouldn't work, and they'd finally have to call the fire department, like when a cat gets stuck in a tree. I suddenly imagine firemen in their suits with masks on, breathing loudly like Darth Vader and edging slowly toward me on their special electric ladder, gloves out, ready to pluck me from my perch.

It's a funny image. It's so funny that unfortunately I start to giggle. Mrs. Abernathy is kind, though, and has a motherly look on her face.

"It's not terribly funny, Gwendolyn. If you need to leave the classroom again, please ask permission before running from the room. You may both get changed and go back to class now."

Oh, I think it's funny. It's hilarious.

I'm going to grow up to be a Thanksgiving Day Parade balloon.

FOURTEEN

I make it through the rest of the day without so much as a hover. I decide it's good that someone else knows what's happening to me. Knowing that Jez knows really helps. She can be my anchor. If I start taking off, she can pull me back to the ground.

It's kind of like that, anyway. She's always the sensible one. Like I said, she's the motherly type, making sure everyone has a sweater and a snack on school trips. Or putting us all to sleep with night-night songs at sleepovers when we were little. Or being the one to call home if one of us is sick or hurt or worried.

I can definitely count on Jez. It makes whatever is happening to me just a little easier to handle.

After school, Jez and I wander along our main street. She doesn't seem to want to talk much; besides, the Chrissies are with us. I have to walk them home and make their dinner on Fridays, since Mom works late. Mom always gives me a little extra money so I can buy us all a treat (Jez included) on

Fridays. We head to The Float Boat, which is the name of the candy store in our town. They make ice cream floats in glasses shaped like boats. Which I guess explains the name.

It's a great place, and you get hit with a sugar smell as soon as you walk in, like every single candy that was ever in there left a little bit of itself behind. Just to tempt you and remind you how delicious it was.

As I stand in front of the store, I get this weird feeling. Float Boat. That's me. I'm a float boat. That's me exactly. Except I'm hardly candy-filled and delicious. I decide then and there that I will think of myself as the "float boat" from now on. It makes me smile.

We walk in. The Chrissies run to the jars filled with jelly beans, like they always do. They never vary much, those two.

There is a whole wall filled with jars of different flavoured jelly beans. Mandarin, lemon, licorice, mint, chocolate, watermelon, vanilla, all the standard flavours. Then all the weird ones that don't associate with any flavour exactly, like midnight sky and winter dream.

What does a "midnight sky" jelly bean taste like, I wonder? But I've never been curious enough to try one. I don't really like jelly beans. I'm more of a chocolate kind of person.

My brother and sister do, though. Every week, the C2s get their jelly bean fix. Christine is very thoroughly going from jar to jar every Friday. Even if the next jar, the jar of the week, is some terrible jelly bean flavour like liverwurst or green pepper (if those exist), she has to take a bag.

Christopher is exactly the opposite. He either picks the same jelly beans every week (he went for an entire year just eating lemon-lime, for instance) or he closes his eyes and points. Whatever jar he points at, he has to try. These days he just grabs different flavours and mixes them up in the same bag (which is fine, since they are all the same price).

This drives his twin sister crazy. She is Miss Jar-a-Week Organized. He is Mr. Any-Jar-Will-Do Random. They are an interesting combination, those two.

As they pick their jelly beans, Jez and I walk up to the counter. Mrs. Forest is standing there with her huge glistening arms and her striped red apron. She is about the biggest lady I've ever seen.

I should tell you a little about Mr. and Mrs. Forest. They own The Float Boat. They are great to us kids. They always remember your birthday and give you extra ice cream if you're in the store that day. Or somehow they know when you aren't having a great day, and they sneak you a little treat you weren't expecting, like your favourite gum drop or something. For me, it's always a Hershey's Kiss.

They don't have any kids of their own, which I think makes them sad. But they sure see enough of everyone else's kids, so it isn't like they don't get to be around any, or anything. I guess if you love kids but can't have any of your own, opening up a candy shop makes a lot of sense.

The kids come to you by the boatload. The floatload.

"Hi, Mrs. Forest," I say. Jez wanders over to the gum balls, daintily picking out a small bag of cinnamon-flavoured ones.

"Hello, Gwennie. Are you ready for a float?" Mrs. Forest says. Then I swear she winks at me.

Now, in a store called The Float Boat, you'd think that's not such an unusual question. It probably wouldn't be for any other kid, any kid other than me.

See, the thing is, I *hate* floats. I always have. I've hated them since the first time I spat one out all over the counter in front of Mr. and Mrs. Forest. I was about four years old, and my dad took me in there and made me try one. And it was hate at first taste. I decided then and there that ice cream and soda had no right to be together in the same glass.

For many years after that, Mrs. Forest would wink at me whenever I was with a bunch of kids and everyone was ordering floats. She'd look over at me and say, "But no float for Miss Gwennie Golden!"

So this was a bit puzzling to me, that suddenly Mrs. Forest was offering me a float.

Especially given the events of the past two days.

Did she want me to spit it out all over the counter? Was she having a quiet day or something and felt the need to clean up a mess of spat-up float?

Since I hesitate, she can sense I'm puzzled. She laughs a little and says quietly, so just I can hear her, "No, no, Miss Gwennie Golden doesn't like floats, does she? But floating, that's a different story."

I snap my head up and look her right in the eye. My face must look really dark and angry, because she raises her eyebrows and whistles.

"Don't get mad, girl. Just come see me when you need me. I'll be here."

Honestly, that's just about the most confusing thing she could say to me. Why would I need to talk to the local candy store owner? What does she know about me? She clearly said "floating."

I want to talk to her then and there. But at that very moment Jez, Christine, *and* Christopher all come up to me. I could tell the twins to go look at something so I can talk more to Mrs. Forest, but I can't get rid of Jez, too. I'll just have to wait to ask her what she meant.

Floating. It's pretty clear that she knows more about me than I do. Just like Mr. McGillies this morning. What's going on with the grownups in this town? She smiles at me and rings up the candy. I pay for everything, and we leave the store. But not before Mrs. Forest calls out to us, "Remember, Gwendolyn. I'm right here."

I nod but frown. I don't say anything, but I'm thinking a lot of things.

Mostly: *Okay, Mrs. Forest. You're right there. You've always been right there, as long as I can remember. What's so important about you being right there now?*

We're all the way home before I realize I'm the only one who didn't buy any candy. It's the first time ever that I left that store empty-handed, but I'm starting to think maybe I'm getting a little old for candy.

FIFTEEN

I have a hard time getting to sleep.

Earlier, I looked everywhere for Mr. McGillies, but it was like he disappeared or something. After I fed them tinned tomato soup, I took the twins and Cassie on her leash, all through our neighbourhood, calling for him. We even went down to the shack by the fields where he lives. It's a place we aren't supposed to go, but it was daytime and this was important.

We walked through our neighbourhood for so long that the Chrissies started to complain. They were tired. They were bored. Why were we looking for dumb old Mr. McGillies anyway? What's so important about him? Cassie liked it, though, she needed a long walk.

But you get the picture.

He just wasn't anywhere, and eventually I had to take the twins home. We sat and watched TV until Mom came home around eight-thirty.

As soon as she came in, I went to bed. To think. Sometimes I have to put the twins to bed, but tonight I just didn't want to. Mom didn't make me.

I read. I toss and turn. I worry. I call Jez but she's asleep and her mom doesn't want to wake her up. I chew my nails.

Finally, just when I think I'll never get to sleep …

… I wake up.

It's really late. It's so late that it's actually probably early the next day. It's bright in my room, because the moon is glowing outside. But that's not what's really important. No, what's more pressing is the fact that my head is gently bump-bumping against my bedroom window.

I wake up floating face down, bumping into my window, like a boat gently bumping into a dock. A float boat.

It's not all that comfortable bumping head first into the window, actually.

I try rolling over, but my body is quite determined. I'm lying on my stomach, banging into the window like a bee trying its darnedest to get out. My body is getting a little more insistent, and the bumping starts to get more forceful.

So I have no choice but to open the window. The glass banging against my head is hurting me, so I think the screen will be better to bang against.

It is, but only a little. It doesn't hurt to bang into the screen, but it's torture of a different kind. I can smell the beautiful spring night. It's warm and smells like new grass and warming dirt. I hear small creatures rustling around out there. The trees are gently waving in the breeze, calling my name.

My body and soul want out the window. My mind isn't so convinced. A force is tugging me outside, a force I can't see, but I sure can feel it. My head starts bulging against the screen and I feel the screen give and tear, just a little. Suddenly I worry that I'm going to break through it, which wouldn't be good.

Panicky. I don't want to go soaring outside. Who knows what could happen? I don't want to fly off into outer space.

I say out loud, "I'll die if I go out there."

Then a voice outside my window says clearly, "No. You won't die, missy."

I know that voice.

It's Mr. McGillies.

SIXTEEN

What is Mr. McGillies doing outside my window at four o'clock in the morning, or whatever time it is?

"Hell … hello?" I stammer.

"It's me, missy. McGovern McGillies."

His first name is McGovern? Who on earth would give their child a first name that started with "Mc" if that was what their last name started with? It was like calling a kid Willie Williams or Robbie Roberts or something. I shake my head.

"Mr. McGillies, what are you doing outside my window?" I call quietly.

"Keeping watch," he says. His voice is coming from below me, on the ground.

Keeping watch? Over what? Are there bad guys out there or something?

"Excuse me, Mr. McGillies, but what are you keeping watch for?" I speak a little louder this time, matching his voice.

"I've been asked by the local authorities to keep watch."

Local authorities? Now, Mr. McGillies isn't exactly a friend to the police. They were always chasing him away from people's garbage and escorting him out of the local restaurants when he got too cranky. They were never mean to him, but not everybody wanted Mr. McGillies and his bottles around, if you know what I mean.

So I ask, "By local authorities, do you mean the police, Mr. McGillies?"

He actually hoots with laughter. "No! My word, missy! Not the police! You know me better than that! Have you ever seen me cozy up to the police in this town?"

My body is actually forcing its way into the window screen now, which is starting to bulge outward. My head feels like it is being squished. It hurts. I'm breathing funny.

I hear Mr. McGillies say, "Relax, missy. Tell your body to act casual. Just think free and easy."

"Okay," I say. "I'm trying to relax. I'm trying to remain calm. But can you please just tell me *why* are you waiting outside my window?"

"I'm watching for a skylark."

"What's a ... what's a skylark?" I ask.

"Oh, I guess that's my special name for a Night Flyer."

Night Flyer?

I shout, desperate: "What's that? What's a Night Flyer, Mr. McGillies?"

But there's no answer.

I begin to wonder if I'm actually asleep and this

is some weird, very strange dream. I pinch myself. Nope, not sleeping.

Then I start to wonder if I'm just really crazy.

I call out the window, "Mr. McGillies? Am I crazy?"

But again it's all quiet out there.

This really worries me, now. A moment before I was speaking to Mr. McGillies the old bottle man outside my window. He was talking about Night Flyers. And now he's not there …

… not good.

I try to think rationally. I'm definitely floating in my bedroom and my head is bulging against the screen. I'm "night flying" right now. It may seem crazy, but I was with Jez and it happened at school today, too, which I guess technically would be "day flying," and Jez is not crazy. These things are true. I'm not asleep.

And if I *am* crazy, why would I imagine an old man I've known forever outside my window? Wouldn't I pick George Washington, or the Queen, or Luke Skywalker or somebody?

Skywalker. Skylark. Sky. Sky. Sky.

I don't know how long I hang here, thinking about Night Flyers, and why Mr. McGillies vanished and whether my mind is just not quite what it should be. I may even fall asleep with these thoughts as my head bumps gently against the window screen.

However long I hang in space drifting in and out of consciousness, in my half-wakeful moments I slowly notice something in front of my nose, something that I've been staring at practically all night …

… my window screen has a tiny brass hook on it. It's on hinges.

My heart skips a beat. Who put a *hook* on the *inside* of my window screen? Only someone who wanted to *get out* of my room!

Before I can stop myself, my hand floats down to the hook and starts playing with it. All I have to do is slip the hook out of the little circle, and the screen will swing open.

My body and I will be free.

I hesitate. My body wants out of this room in the worst way. My head says maybe that isn't such a great idea, but my body is just shaking all over. I'm just trembling with excitement from top to bottom. Now I know that I can get out of my room, I'm feeling a kind of full-body desire that I can't say is all that great. My palms are sweaty. My arms and legs are on fire. My heart is pounding. Every ounce of my body wants out. My old head is very concerned, though.

Will I be safe out there?

It's a little like when you stand on the edge of a cliff, and a tiny, crazy voice in your head whispers, "What would happen if you jump?" You really don't want to jump, and some louder, saner voice says, "Don't be stupid, not a great idea." But because that little voice went and spoke up, you're stuck listening to it, and it gets louder.

I think for a few more moments. Then what do I do?

I jump.

Before I can stop myself, I unlatch the hook and the screen squeaks open gently. The next moment, my body takes off.

It just takes off. That's the pure truth. My body just zooms out that window, and I can't stop it even if I want to.

But I don't want to.

I'm soaring, and there is nothing but midnight sky, beautiful sky, between me and the stars.

SEVENTEEN

My body just flies me as high and far as it can, as fast as it can. It's like when you let the air out of a balloon, and it just flies all over the place with no particular plan. For a moment I'm so high up I can see our whole town, and the melting place between the edge of town and the dark empty fields ready for sowing corn, all below me. Way off in the distance I see a bright glow on the horizon. It's the city, a place I've never been.

My body stops long enough for me to notice how huge the world is, how dark and how much is waiting for me, too.

It's powerful but terrifying.

The second thing my body does is take me over to the trees, where I whiz and spin and fly through them. Somehow I don't hit any branches or leaves, but they are touching my feet, my hands, as I whiz by. I can smell the trees, the smell they make in the night. It's like secrets, and green.

I'm whirring all over those trees. I see stars, then

sky, then the moon, then stars again. I'm flashing all over the place, like a butterfly or a hummingbird.

Or a bat.

Then my body takes me low, really low, so I buzz over the grass and I can smell dirt and lawn and flowers. I buzz over the neighbours' flowerbeds and make their bushes and tall yellow flowers swirl and dance with the air I stir as I blow by.

Before I know it, I whiz three lawns over and I get the fright of my life: a giant snarling dog leaps out of his dog house and up into my face. I almost get my face bitten off. Flecks of dog spit actually hit me in the mouth. I know this killer dog lives in this yard, but in the excitement of the moment, I just forgot about him. He misses me but leaps up again and again, snapping at my heels as I try to escape. My heart is pounding. For a terrible second I feel myself slowly sinking, as I stare down at my toes getting closer and closer to that stupid, snarling, snapping dog.

This is not the moment to stop flying, body! Move IT! I shriek to myself. I can feel his heat and his rage, and it scares me. That scare gets my heart pumping, and my legs start kicking and my arms start flailing, and I zoom over his head. Luckily no one in the house wakes up, and I escape.

I fly away as fast as I can without any real direction in mind. That was just too close. That dog is known to kill things, cats and rabbits, mostly. Cassie refuses to go anywhere near the house whenever I take her for a walk.

How could I be so forgetful? I feel like dumb luck just helped me escape a great harm. I have to pay more attention here.

I fly to my roof, hovering near the chimney, when suddenly I feel dizzy and sick.

I hang on to the chimney, because I think I'm going to throw up, for real. Stupid dog. I suddenly want *down*. I hang on to the chimney for all I'm worth. I peek between my toes to the grass below me: I'm a *long way up* and I'm sweaty and panicky, and I can't fly and my body feels like a lead weight. I think I'm just about to die ...

... when suddenly a voice right beside my head says, "Hi, Gwennie Golden. How do you like floating now?"

But this time it isn't Mr. McGillies. Oh, no. This time it's the warm, beautiful voice of Mrs. Forest.

I must be hallucinating.

I turn my sweaty head toward the warm voice, but I'm too scared and sick to say anything and my eyes are closed tight so I can't see anything either. I'm just covered in sweat now, and shaky. My arms are about to give out and I'm going to fall ... when Mrs. Forest puts her big arms around me and says, "Okay now, Gwennie, how about you just carefully let go of that chimney, and we get you safely onto the roof?"

The warmth of her body, her closeness, even the faint smell of sweet candy on her skin is awfully real for a hallucination. I turn my head into her shoulder and mumble, "M ... mmm ... Mrs. Forest, is that you?" just like a little kid. I unsqueeze my eyes just a little, and there she is in all her big glory. I let go of the chimney, and she lays me on the roof so gently that in my state I think for a moment that she's an angel.

My dark angel.

"Mrs. Forest?" I pant, lying there and staring at the starlit sky. I feel so sick. My head is swirling around and I'm all sweaty. My pyjamas cling to me, even though it isn't a boiling hot night or anything. I start shivering and shuddering.

"Yes, honey?" she says calmly. She's digging in a backpack she must have brought along and pulls out a warm blanket, which she puts over me. I'm instantly happier. Then I hear her rummaging some more in her backpack, and I smell chamomile tea. She pours hot tea from a flask into the little plastic lid and helps me sit up to take a sip.

"Mrs. Forest, is that really y-y-you?" My teeth are chattering. This surprises me: they really do chatter, like people say.

"Yes, Gwennie, it's me," she answers, sitting on the roof beside me. She groans softly as she lowers her big body to the roof. Her warmth moves from her and along to me, just a little.

She seems pretty convincingly real.

"How did you get here?" I ask. After the sip of tea, I feel a little less sick and look around. We're a long way up, on the top of my house, looking out over the whole neighbourhood. The sky is slightly pink in the east. The sun is coming.

"Mr. McGillies came to get me," she answers matter-of-factly.

"Mr. McGillies?" I'm confused then remember that I was talking to him earlier. "Well, I mean, how did you get up here, on my roof?"

Then she says something very softly. "Look around, Gwennie. Do you see a ladder or anything? It's five o'clock in the morning. We're sitting on your roof. How did *you* get up here? How do you think *I* got up here?"

I swallow my tea and pull the blanket over my shoulders. I decide not to speak, because whatever I say will sound crazy and I'm tired of it. I'm still half convinced this is a dream. Maybe I'm coming down with something.

"I'm not going to tell you how I got up here, because it'll sound crazy, but I think you know how you got up here, Mrs. Forest. Okay, no ladder then. But how *are* we going to get down?"

"Like I said, the same way we got up here."

She looks straight through me with her dark, dark eyes. She isn't smiling.

Very quietly she says, "We fly."

EIGHTEEN

I stare back at her, stunned. I simply can't think of a thing to say that doesn't sound like I'm insane or stuck in a Disney movie, or perhaps both. She sounds a little crazy too, actually. I run my hand over my forehead to check for a fever.

Nope, no illness that I can detect.

"We fly down, because we're Night Flyers, Gwen," Mrs. Forest repeats calmly. She doesn't stop staring at me when she says it, so I can see that she's not kidding.

I want to say something sensible, but what comes out from behind my thick, stupid tongue is: "You are, too? Flyer? I'm a what?" Clearly, on the outside I'm not sounding terribly bright.

Things are making a bit more sense on the inside, though. I'm thinking: *Oh, I see.* Other *girls just get to have their period. I get to have my period* and *start flying around the neighbourhood, too. That's me all right. That's just so me.*

I shuffle under the blanket. I really don't want any part of this, or any more to do with this crazy night.

Mrs. Forest is head down, rummaging in her backpack, then she pulls out a dusty, very battered-looking book. She blows on it and dust actually flows off it into the night air toward me. I cough.

She hands it to me. "You should read this."

It's big, this book. It will take me forever to read, and I'm not much of a reader. The cover says *Your First Flight: A Night Flyer's Handbook*. There's an illustration of a kid on it, a little younger than me, holding hands between his parents. They look like a totally normal family walking along the street together, except they aren't walking. They're flying, and all three look very happy about it, like in whatever universe they inhabit, people fly around over their neighbours' heads all the time.

I lay the book on the roof beside me. I sigh. I'm suddenly so weary I could fall asleep sitting right here. I start flying around in my room, at school, outside, and now there's a huge book I have to read about it, too. How is that fair?

"Mrs. Forest, I just want to go to bed. How are we *really* going to get down?"

"I told you, Gwennie, the same way we got up here. We fly. And we got to go. It's getting light out." Mrs. Forest is speaking very gently, almost too quietly for me to hear. Maybe she doesn't want me to freak out, so she's saying it like she would to a little kid. She is gathering the flask, the blanket, the handbook, and putting everything into her backpack. She's moving really slowly, like she doesn't want to startle me. She shoulders the backpack and I get the message: it's time to go.

She helps me stand up. My legs are really wobbly, but the tea made me feel a little better. As we stand up, I see Mr. McGillies way down on the ground below me. He waves up at me, then turns and trundles his cart away down the street, noisy in the quiet. I raise my hand in reply, but don't have the strength to wave.

"What's he doing?" I ask.

"His job," she answers.

"His j-jobbbb?" I ask. My teeth are chattering again.

"He's looking out for you because it's his job. He's a Watcher."

"A Watcher?"

"Yes, he watches. Quiet now, child. Shh." She is busy shifting her backpack, preoccupied.

"Mrs. Forest, why am I so cold?"

"It's part of the First Flight, Gwen. Most people don't go by themselves the first time, because it's a big shock to the system. The handbook tells you what you need to know. Right now we have to get you back into your bedroom before the whole town wakes up." She's right — the sky is getting lighter and lighter.

Mrs. Forest takes a look over the edge of the rooftop, then turns and takes me by the shoulders and looks into my face. She's stern.

"You're recovered enough to fly back down. Now, this is important. You don't let go of my hand, okay? We're just going to float really slow, gentle, back down to your window. You're not going to think of anything, you're not going to ask any questions, you're going to breathe slowly and imagine being safely back in your bed. Thoughts count here, Gwen. Okay?"

I nod. I feel myself start to break into a sweat again. I hold her hand, and there's no way for me to tell you the courage it takes to step off that roof back into the air. My knees are weak. I'm breathing fast but Mrs. Forest says, "Slow down your breathing, Gwen, tell your body to calm down."

I tell myself to calm down, and immediately I feel better. I feel a rush of gladness that my body is listening to me for once. If this is going to work at all, my body and my mind are going to have to start to work together here.

The first step is the hardest. We sink fast, me clutching Mrs. Forest's hand, but then she buoys me up. We float, slowly, like a maple key gently spinning from the treetops. I keep my eyes closed, and I think I'm going to throw up, but I don't. I feel the air gently moving against my skin, and in a few moments I hear the screen on my window creak open. Mrs. Forest gently pushes me through the window and I float into my room and over to my bed like an obedient balloon.

"Goodnight, Gwen. You have to sleep now. We'll talk tomorrow. Think of lying down on your bed," she commands quietly. I think about my soft covers, and slowly my body sinks into the bed. I pull the covers over my head. I hear her place the handbook on the floor under my bed, close the window, and shut the screen, then Mrs. Forest is gone.

My mind is a jumble of thoughts, which mostly revolve around something like: *I'm a Night Flyer. I had my First Flight. Mrs. Forest can fly, too.*

Just before I fall asleep I have one more thought clear as a bell: I'm *never* going to be able to read that big handbook from cover-to-cover.

Ever.

NINETEEN

You'd think that after a night like that, I'd lie wide awake worrying, or at least wondering about myself.

But I don't. As soon as my head hits the pillow, I fall into the deepest sleep of my life. I don't dream either. I just sleep, and sleep, and sleep some more.

I wake up really late, in my bed and not on the ceiling for the first time since this began. Mom must have let me sleep in. The sun is blazing into my room like a sun lamp, shining right on my face. Cassie is sitting looking at me, whining. That's what finally wakes me up.

She needs to go out to go pee. She has that look on her face.

I roll over and listen. The house is quiet, so my mom and the twins are out. They probably let me sleep in while they went out for pancakes. It's a regular Saturday family date, but these days I don't go with them very often.

Or at least not as often as I used to. Sometimes Mom makes me go, and sometimes she doesn't.

Today, she doesn't, which is probably just as well. I have a lot to think about, and it's pretty much impossible to think at breakfast with the twins. And besides, I'm still not sure I won't start floating around at the Pancake House, which would be quite interesting for the Saturday morning pancake crowd, maybe, but not so great for me.

Cassie whines again, licks her nose, and wiggles. She really has to go, and I don't want to start the day by cleaning up one of her accidents. I really don't want to start the day by tackling the handbook either, but even if I want to I can't. I have to get up and do my paper route.

"Okay, okay, let's go," I say. I am feeling pretty great, though. Once again, I wake up with tons of energy, even though I was up so late, or early, that I barely got any sleep at all. It takes some getting used to.

Cassie roars out the bedroom door ahead of me and hustles downstairs. My dog is a little overweight and getting on in dog years, so you can hear her thump on every stair she goes down.

She is waiting beside the front door when I get there. I manage to put on some shorts and a T-shirt. I don't worry too much about my hair, since I never do. I take down her leash then grab a banana and a juice box. I know I'm way too old to be drinking from a juice box, but they are in the fridge on account of the Chrissies, and I have to admit, they do come in handy.

Then we head outside. It is without a doubt the most beautiful morning I ever remember. The sun is shining, it's not too hot, and the fruit trees are all out in full bloom. The lilac trees are waving in the morning sunlight, and even the grass is greener than usual. The town looks clean and fresh and smells great, like it just got out of a hot bath and got scrubbed fresh all over.

But now I have a secret about my town. I can love it in the daytime, like everyone else. And I can love it at night, too, when no one else is around. I know what everyone's front lawn looks like from the treetops, because I've been there. I know what gardens, and cars, and the street, and the neighbour's rooftop looks like, because I'm the float boat and I've seen it all from a fresh new point of view, like a bird sees it. I'll never look at crows the same way.

I go to the bottom of the driveway and pull open my bag of papers to deliver. It's the local newspaper, filled with stories about the high-school hockey team or retiring police officers. That kind of stuff. I roll and stack them in my old wagon, then I tie Cassie's leash to the handle and we go along the street to deliver papers. Every Saturday morning I remember that I'm a little old to be pulling a wagon, and I should really save up for a buggy like everybody else.

I toss a paper to the first house: Mrs. Alpen. (She's old and likes to rock in her armchair on the front porch. She's there now. I wave, but she doesn't. She never does. I always wave, anyway, hoping one day she'll surprise me and wave back.)

I flew last night.

I toss the second paper to the next house: Mr. and Mrs. Peter Shanly. (He's the local dentist, she's got a load of kids to look after, five and counting.)

I flew last night, because I am a Night Flyer, or a skylark, or whatever you want to call me.

I toss the third paper: Mal Pete. (He is really Malcolm Pete and hates being called "Mal" but the label on the newspaper was typed in wrong and they never fixed it. *Mal* means "sick" in French.)

I can fly.

I keep tossing papers all morning and keep talking to myself about what happened to me.

What's happening to me. The more I say it to myself, the easier it is to say. And the easier it is to say, the truer it seems.

I'm a Night Flyer. A skylark. I can fly.

After I deliver all the papers, I take my wagon back to my street, and I see Mr. McGillies coming toward me pushing his crazy bottle cart. He's humming to himself. When he gets close enough I say, "Hey, Mr. McGillies!" but he just keeps on walking like he doesn't hear me.

I try again, louder this time. "Hey, Mr. McGillies, over here. It's me, Gwennie!" I really want to add, "You know, the skylark," but I don't. He knows. It would be kind of nice to say out loud, though.

But again, it's like he doesn't hear me. So I run over to him, dragging my wagon and Cassie behind me, and stop in front of him.

"Hey, Mr. McGillies, it's me, Gwennie, the skylark," I say, quietly.

But he just looks at me and blinks. "Gwennie? Gwennie? Not sure who you are, ma'am, but you're in my way!" He pushes past me with his shopping cart rattling.

Now, that's odd. That's very odd. Mr. McGillies has always said hello to me before, every day of my life, if I say hello to him first.

So I run up to him again, and say, "Hey. What's wrong with you? It's me. Gwennie Golden! The girl from this street!"

I'm a little mad and suddenly a bit scared. Why is he pretending he doesn't know who I am?

He stops and looks at me. Then he says really slow, "I don't see any *girl* named Gwennie. I just see a whole new *grown-up* person named Gwendolyn. Pleased to meet you, ma'am." He looks at me steadily and I must look like I'm going to cry, because I see him wink.

It takes just a second, but it's enough to remind me that I haven't changed so much.

I'm a Night Flyer who had her first flight, and I'm Gwendolyn. But I'm still Gwennie. I'm not changed so much from yesterday.

His wink tells me that. I'm growing up. Grown up. But not so much. Not yet.

Not so you wouldn't recognize me.

TWENTY

I put my wagon in the hut at the back of the house, and I take Cassie and me in for some lunch.

Now this is not like a big deal or anything, and I don't want to make too much of it, but when I go to the bathroom, I get my period.

It isn't the first time, but it's still new enough that I'm surprised at first. Mom got me some pads the last time, so I know what to do. I get cleaned up and go and watch TV, eating tinned chicken soup. Cassie joins me on the couch and falls asleep snoring against my leg.

My head is spinning a little. I want to talk more to Mrs. Forest, but I also don't want to go outside. It's hot out there now, and I'm starting to feel a little headachy.

I want to ask Mrs. Forest a lot more questions: Do I have to fly every night? When am I going to get some sleep? Does anyone else in the neighbourhood fly around too? The police chief? The librarian? Any of my teachers? The thought of Mr. Marcus floating around at night along with me gives me the creeps.

Do I have any say in this at all?

I think about the giant handbook upstairs under my bed. I *know* I should go and start reading it, but I'm too comfortable curled up on the couch with Cassie to move. Truth is, I'm a little worried about that handbook. What if it tells me something I don't want to know? It looks so out-of-date too, how can it really be about me? I put it off.

And honestly, I'm not exactly the world's strongest reader, even with skinny books. The sheer size of that book just worries me.

My mom and the twins come home around two o'clock in the afternoon. I'm sort of dozing on the couch and jump up when they come in.

The Chrissies roar past me with huge ice cream cones dripping down their arms, without saying hello.

My mom comes in and kisses my head then looks worried. She runs her hand over my forehead like she did whenever I had a fever when I was little.

"Gwen, are you feeling okay?" she asks. "You're pale as a ghost." She hands me a huge cup of chocolate chip ice cream as she says this, which does a lot to improve my mood.

"I'm okay. I'm a little tired," I say as I take the wooden spoon that comes with the ice cream and shovel a spoonful into my mouth. The ice cream is good and cool and sweet. I lower my voice. "I just got my period." It's kind of a new thing for me to say to my mom, and it still feels a little weird.

She nods and says, "Oh," like it makes a lot of sense. "Well, come help me unload the groceries, then you can go out with Jez if you want," she adds.

She hugs me and doesn't say anything more. I want to say, "Mom, I need to tell you something else," but I just don't know how.

How do you tell your mother you can fly?

It's probably going to come up, but I just don't know how to start that conversation.

So I don't.

TWENTY-ONE

I call Jez, but she's going to a family barbecue. Jez comes from a huge family. Not at home — there it's just her and her mom. But her mom has eight brothers and sisters, and Jez has twenty-nine first cousins or something. Enough people that someone is always having a barbecue or a family picnic or some get-together, every Saturday.

"Do you want to come?" she asks me, but I say no, I'll see her later. Sometimes I go along, but I just don't feel like it today. I just don't feel like being with a lot of people who don't know I'm a Night Flyer.

I really just want to talk to Mrs. Forest. And then there's the handbook, which is beginning to nag at me, like a chore I have to do.

So after I help Mom with the groceries, and I put everything on the shelf, and I wash up the Chrissies (who are sticky and completely covered in ice cream), I ask my mom if I can go out. I tell her I want to go to the library and maybe the Float Boat.

"The library? Okay, sure. But you just had a big ice cream, so no candy at the Float Boat."

My mom helps me find my library card (which is hidden behind the Chrissies' book shelf, since they were playing "let's go to the library" with it some time ago). I go into my room and stick my head under my bed: there's a Hershey's Kiss sitting on top of the handbook. Nice touch, Mrs. Forest, but candy-coating isn't going to help me digest this gigantic book any easier. Or faster.

I unwrap the Kiss and pop it in my mouth, then shove the handbook into my backpack. It's surprisingly light. Mom tells me to be home in time for dinner and I leave.

She's right to be surprised about the library.

I'm not exactly the most academic person in the world. But I do go to the library sometimes. We don't have a computer, so if I need one, I use one at the library. I have to admit, that's usually the only reason I go there. But this time I want to go to the library because if I'm caught reading a book in my bedroom, everyone will be so ecstatic that I'll have to show them what I'm reading. I really don't want my mom to catch me reading *Your First Flight: A Night Flyer's Handbook*.

The library just seems safer.

It's late in the afternoon, and I walk slowly along the quiet streets. There's no one around, probably because it's suddenly so hot and people aren't used to it yet. I walk by the Float Boat and stick my head in the front door, but there's no sign of Mrs. Forest, just Mr. Forest. And he's busy with a huge mass of kids who all want floats.

"Hi, Mr. Forest!" I call out.

"Hi, Gwen!" he calls back over the kids' heads.

"Is Mrs. Forest here?" I call out again.

"No, sorry, Gwen, she had to leave on an emergency visit to see her sister in Napanee until tomorrow. She told me to tell you she'll see you then," he calls, then gets lost in a sea of children all yelling out their float orders. I see him reach beneath the counter, though, and he pulls out an envelope. He raises it above his head. "She left this for you," he says. I can see that he can't possibly get through all those kids, so I wade in and grab it from him.

"Thanks, Mr. Forest," I say, pushing little children aside, but those kids are so loud I don't think he hears me. The envelope says, GWENDOLYN G. on the outside, in very neat capital letters.

Outside, I tear it open, and it says, *Dear Gwen, I'm called out of town for a day or two, sorry. Look at the handbook, tell your body what to do, remember to breathe, stay safe. If anything happens, find Mr. McGillies. I'll see you as soon as I get back. And it's probably best if you don't go out flying alone, at least for now. Yours, Emmeline Forest.*

I'm thinking two things. The first is: *Emmeline? What a pretty name.*

The second is: *Mrs. Forest has gone out of town! What the heck am I going to do without her?*

I try to stay calm. It's okay. I'll be okay. I know

a thing or two now about controlling my breathing, telling my body what to do.

So I continue to the library. For a spring day, it's way too hot.

At the library (which is nice and cool), I find a computer far away from everyone else. I know I should start reading the handbook, but I don't. I just wonder what I'll find on the computer, so I check there first. I'm lazy, it's true. I flop into the chair and I type in: "Night Flyers."

I'm not sure what I'm going to find.

There's some stuff on bats, sure that makes sense. "Nature's Night Fliers." Interesting that there seem to be two spellings for the word "flyers."

There's some stuff on World War II fighter pilots and warplanes. They were night flyers too, I guess.

There is a bad-looking vampire movie called *Monster Night Flier*, and then a mystery about birds with the same name.

Nothing about humans flying at night, though, at least not without being a vampire or having an airplane underneath them.

Not really surprising.

So then I type in "night walker," and a bunch of stuff pops up. It's all about sleepwalking. There's a lot on sleepwalking, that's for sure. Pages of it. I find out that sleepwalking was first written about two thousand years ago. That it has another name that I can't pronounce, which is spelled "s-o-m-n-a-m-b-u-l-i-s-m," and that it affects up to fifteen people in one hundred.

I do some quick math: our town has about two thousand people in it, so that would mean about three hundred sleepwalkers, give or take a few.

How many Night Flyers are there? I suddenly wonder. Somehow I don't think we have three hundred Night Flyers in town. The sky would have been full of people floating all over the place and bumping into each other last night, if there were that many of us. So far as I know, it's just Mrs. Forest and me. I'll have to ask her about that when I see her tomorrow. The list of questions I want to ask that woman is just getting longer and longer.

The library is getting quieter and emptier as people leave for home. I really have to open my handbook, so I go find a lonesome reading chair, as far from everyone as I can get. I take the clumsy book out of my pack and just stare at it. It's really dusty. The family on the front cover is so old-fashioned it's almost laughable. They're from the 1950s or something, the little boy with shorts and a shirt with a bow tie, the dad in a dark business suit and shiny shoes, the mom in a pretty flowered dress and high heels and pearls around her neck.

And they're all flying so happily along.

I just know I'm never going to read this book. I've never read anything longer than a pamphlet about summer camp. But I should at least open the front cover, because I know that even if I don't read a word, the first thing Mrs. Forest is going to ask me the next time I see her is if I've opened it yet.

I open the front cover. And stare.

The book is cut away on the inside so it's really a box that just looks like a book from the outside. It's not a book at all.

And inside the box are three items.

The first item is a creamy yellow envelope with "Gwendolyn Golden, N.F." typed on it.

The second is a small, colourful brochure with the headline *Your Life as a Night Flyer Starts Today*. It has a subhead: *Your 10 Most Pressing Questions Answered*. There is a red slash across the side of the brochure cover that reads *Micro-Edition for the Less-than-Willing Reader*.

I smile at this. Someone has me figured out. I feel a tiny bit reassured. I'm less-than-willing, all right, about most things in life.

The third item in the box is a beautiful golden feather, made of bright, light metal. It reminds me of the aluminum foil that Mom sometimes uses for wrapping up baked potatoes, except it's gold and shaped like a feather.

I open the envelope with my name on it first. It's made of heavy paper and feels old and expensive. The typed letter inside is short:

> *Dear Ms. Gwendolyn I. Golden,*
> *Congratulations on the successful completion of your First Flight. You are now a Night Flyer with full privileges (see Appendix D, details attached). Your Mentor, Mrs. Emmeline Beatrice Forest, and your Watcher, Mr. McGovern Everett*

McGillies the Third, have been notified.
Best regards from the Flight Crew, Local 749

That's it.

I read this letter probably fifty times (since it's so short). All I really get from it though is that Mrs. Forest has a great name, and Mr. McGillies has a terrible one. And what on earth is Local 749?

So I turn my attention to the little brochure, *Your Life as a Night Flyer Starts Today.* I am ridiculously relieved, and a little ashamed, to be honest. A three-page brochure that answers my *10 Most Pressing Questions* is something I can probably read from beginning to end without too much trouble. Although now I'm slightly annoyed at being pegged as a Less-than-Willing Reader. Why do other kids get an eight-hundred-page book and I just get this little brochure?

Honestly, I'm never satisfied.

The picture on the front cover of the brochure is interesting. It's a girl about my age flying beside a huge old tree. It's night, and there is a hint of something glowing behind her, but you can't see what. And she looks happy. Like really, really happy. Full of joyousness, if that's a word.

I open the cover. The ten questions are neatly laid out:

1. *What is happening to me?*
2. *What is a Night Flyer?*
3. *Is Night Flying dangerous?*

4. *How do I control my flying?*
5. *How do I tell my friends?*
6. *What is a Watcher?*
7. *What is a Mentor?*
8. *What Ceremonies and Parties do I attend?*
9. *Can I lead a normal life?*
10. *How many Night Flyers are there?*

I read the first question:

#1: What is happening to me?
You are in all probability a young teenager from a family of Night Flyers (except in very rare circumstances), and you have recently flown without mechanical assistance, which means that you have had your First Flight. You have therefore been identified by local authorities (see Mentor and Watcher entries, below) as a Night Flyer. Rest assured that you are normal in every way, except now you have the added ability of unaided flight.

This is going to be helpful, obviously. "*Normal in every way,*" sounds good to me, except I can already see that it's going to lead to a lot more questions. I'm not from a family of Night Flyers, so apparently I'm a rare specimen right from the first sentence.

I scan a little. The answer to question five would have been useful a few days ago:

#5: How do I tell my friends?
In most cases, the Night Flyer need not tell anyone except family members and other Flyers about his or her new ability. The decision to tell non-flying friends and community members must be made very carefully, and often is not recommended. This is because in many, many unfortunate cases, non-flying prejudice has occurred. Extreme caution and restraint is advised, although there are no rules which forbid revealing the truth. Seek advice and wisdom from your Mentor.

I'm just not sure how much *extreme caution* I can manage. And Jez knows the truth, so that's one strongly worded caution from the Flight Crew that I've already ignored. Not a great start, really.

I skip down to the entries about the Watcher and the Mentor.

#6: What is a Watcher?
One who watches, keeps watch, or is especially vigilant as a sentry or night guard. S/he is someone who is well-known to the Flyer, and who is constantly on the lookout for his or her First Flight, and continued welfare. The Watcher is generally a Flyer themselves, but this is not essential. The Watcher and Mentor must work together well. The Watcher must take an oath to Watch faithfully.

Is Mr. McGovern Everett McGillies the Third up to this job? An *oath*? The only oath that comes to mind when I think of Mr. McGillies is a not-very-nice swear word, which he tends to use a lot.

And *watch faithfully*? I suddenly wonder if the people in charge here have ever actually *met* Mr. McGillies?

The Mentor entry is a little more reassuring:

#7: What is a Mentor?
A Mentor is steadfast, honourable, courageous. S/he is there to teach, guide, and help the young Night Flyer in every facet of his or her learning. The Mentor is not, in most cases, a family member, but is instead a member of the young Flyer's community. The Mentor/First Flyer relationship is usually one of great respect which often lasts into adulthood and beyond. The Mentor must take an oath to teach and guide faithfully. It is a sacred trust.

I think of all the times Mrs. Emmeline Beatrice Forest has smiled at me in The Float Boat over the years. Where her smile found me in a pile of squealing kids and made me feel like she knew I was there, regardless of whether we spoke to each other or not. I think about her finding me on the roof last night.

I somehow know she won't fail me.

I turn the brochure over, and there on the back is Appendix D (what happened to A, B, and C, I wonder?).

Here is what it says:

Your Life as a Night Flyer Starts Today:
Appendix D

5 Full Privileges of a Night Flyer:
1. *You may now fly unrestricted, day* or night, at your discretion. (*Daytime flight is generally not recommended in populated areas)*
2. *You have received your golden feather. You will receive only one. Keep it safe.*
3. *You now have a Watcher and Mentor who have each taken an oath on your behalf.*
4. *You may attend all Night Flying ceremonies as a Member with Full Privileges (see Question #8, reverse).*
5. *You must choose.*

Numbers one through four are reasonably clear, or I figure I can piece them together with the ten questions and help from Mrs. Forest. But number five throws me.

You must choose.

Choose what? I feel fairly certain that this is going to come up again, soon.

I put the brochure back into the handbook for later and pick up the golden feather. It's a really special thing, light to the touch, but you can tell it's strong, too, strong as metal. It's tough and beautiful. I'm looking at it up close when I hear someone come up behind me. I spin around.

It's Martin Evells. I stow the golden feather, slam the handbook shut, and stuff it into my backpack.

"Hi, Gwen," he says and smiles at me. It's a great smile. It's always been a favourite of mine. "What are you reading?" he asks politely.

"Hi, Martin. Um, just an old book about night … flying … creatures," I manage to spit out. I'm clearly not too quick on the uptake.

I stand up and sling my backpack over my shoulder. My body literally leaps up and gets all trembly. My arms and legs start prickling like they are on fire. Uh-oh.

"Um, we're having an end-of-year party tonight at my house," he says. He says it really quickly, all running together, so I can hardly make out what he's saying.

"My mom is setting up a food table and we're playing music. I hope you can come." He says this like it would be really nice if I showed up.

My finger starts to float, just a little. I snap my hand shut. My foot starts to lift off the floor, just a tiny bit. I slam it down, hard. I remember what Mrs. Forest said to me last night, "Just tell your body what to do, Gwen. It'll listen, it has to."

I tell my body, *Just quit it. No one wants to see you flying around the library ceiling like a bat or a World War II fighting airplane. Just get a grip.*

I say to Martin, "That sounds really nice, Martin. Can I bring a friend?"

He says sure, please do. He tells me where he lives (like I don't remember from all those play dates we had when we were little), and says he'll see me later.

I nod. I tell him I'll see him later, too.

Apparently I'm going to a party at Martin Evells' house tonight. And I'm a Night Flyer. And Mrs. Emmeline Beatrice Forest, my Mentor, is out of town. Mr. McGovern Everett McGillies the Third, my Watcher, is probably around somewhere, but he's not exactly the most reliable person in the world.

Still, I should probably be grateful for whatever help I can get.

I'm not entirely sure how this is going to work out. I seem to have more control of myself in the day-time, which is a huge relief and I'm not complaining about that.

But what about at night? Last night wasn't exactly a great start to this whole Night Flying thing.

I know two things for sure, though.

One: I am *not* going to miss out on Martin's party.

Two: I really am not sure what's going to happen tonight, or if I am ready to fly solo, if it comes to that.

TWENTY-TWO

I walk home in the golden late afternoon. I'm just skimming along, although my feet are very firmly planted on the ground with every step. I have this floaty feeling, but it has nothing to do with my body.

No, this time the floaty feeling is all inside my stomach, which feels like it might actually be inhabited by about a million little butterflies.

I'm not sure how to tell my mom I'm invited to a party. It just isn't something that happens a lot in my town, not to kids my age. It's the first time I've been invited to a party that didn't come with a little paper invitation with balloons or puppies on it. Knowing my mom, she'll want to know the time and place and who's going, and she'll call Martin's mom and maybe be mortifying and drop me off at the front door. That wouldn't be good.

What if she calls it a "play date"?

I gulp. A certain kind of panic starts to take hold of me.

I open the front door, and it's cool and quiet inside. I tiptoe into the kitchen and just about jump out of my skin when my mom is sitting quietly at the kitchen table reading a magazine. I actually clutch my chest.

"Mom, jeesh, you almost gave me a heart attack! You're so quiet! Where's C2?" I ask. I grab an apple from the fruit bowl on the counter, shine it up, and take a bite. Usually my mom would say something about the C2 remark, something gentle but firm like, "You know their names, Gwendolyn, please use them," but this time she doesn't.

Instead she says, "They're at a friend's house for a few hours. I thought I'd take a minute to myself. Do you want a cup of tea?" My mom smiles at me. She's pretty. I like the way she looks. I have green eyes and long dark hair, just like her.

I chew big chomps of my apple but realize that I must look and sound exactly like a horse, so I stop. I'm going to have to start working on being a little more ladylike.

"Mom, I got invited to a party, at Martin Evells' place. Tonight." I say this as casually as I can. Please don't let her look all excited and proud like she does when I get a phone call from someone other than Jez. Please don't let her jump up and grab the phone and call Martin's mom for details like when me and Martin were little.

But she doesn't do anything. She just closes her magazine and put her hands on her knees, really still. She smiles.

"That's nice. You were really good friends with Martin once. Best friends, when you were little. Are you going to go?"

I think my mouth might be open a little, so I close it. I swallow some apple remnants. She's asking me. I'm being given a choice here.

I pause and shrug. "I want to go … he's always been nice to me … we *were* really good friends once …." I start to say, then I get all loopy and my eyes well up with tears and suddenly I really don't know why, but I'm crying all over the place and my mom is hugging me and telling me it's fine and that I don't have to go, but it will probably be really fun and maybe I should go, even for just a little bit. She says that maybe it's time for Martin and me to be friends again.

And maybe I should just take a bowl of ice cream up to my room and think about it.

My mom gives me a ton of tissue and a huge bowl of chocolate ice cream. But as soon as she hands me the ice cream my tears stop, honestly just like a little kid.

Weird. Very weird. I haven't cried in ages, I think I said that. I haven't cried in so long, I can't really remember the last time.

And then, boom, I do a little night flying, I get my period, an old friend from when I was a kid shows me some kindness and invites me to a party, and I'm crying all over the place.

I couldn't say exactly why, but that cry in the kitchen with my mom hugging me made me feel better. My mom dries my eyes and says mom stuff like I'm a great kid, and it's hard changing into a teenager, and everybody feels uncomfortable and weird and different at this time in their life.

If she only knew how truly weird and different I am.

I take my backpack, my ice cream, and the tissue box and go up to my room. I take the handbook out and stow it safely under my bed, under some clothes so no one can see it. Then I open my cupboard and start to think about what I'm going to wear.

Which poses a whole new set of problems and makes me want to cry again, but for a different reason. My wardrobe isn't exactly brimming with this year's latest looks, if you know what I mean.

But more importantly, just what, exactly, does a Night Flyer wear to a party?

I need help, fast.

TWENTY-THREE

I need Jez. But I forgot: she's at a family barbecue.

Rats. What am I going to do? I'm on my own.

I stand in front of my open closet. Lots of brown corduroys and black leggings. My shirts are all purple and dark brown. There are some horrifying cutesy dresses that I stopped wearing a few years ago but haven't gotten around to moving into Christine's closet.

My wardrobe looks like a giant bruise. When was the last time I went shopping for clothes? I do a mental memory check, and it doesn't really compute. It must have been over a year ago. Apart from a few essentials, lately I've been mostly borrowing Mom's stuff.

I'm just about to go down to the kitchen to see if Mom can help when she knocks on the door. She's been doing that a lot more lately, knocking instead of just walking in.

"Come in," I say.

She walks in with a box with a ribbon on it. Ribbons don't figure particularly large in our lives, not even at

Christmas, so I'm suddenly a little edgy and worried.

She laughs. "Don't panic, Gwennie. It's not a pink satin dress or anything. I bought this for your birthday next month, but you might want to try it out tonight."

My mom takes the lid off the box, and there inside is the most beautiful long swishy shirt I've ever seen. It's dark green with white pearl buttons up the front, and I think it's made of silk or something really soft.

I instantly love it and pick it up and rub it against my face.

Night Flyer or not, my mom does know me a little, I guess.

"Thanks, Mom," is all I can say. She nods and gives my shoulder a squeeze.

"You can borrow my leather sandals, too, if you like," are her parting words as she turns and vanishes through the door.

Her leather sandals cost $150 at the store in the big town down the highway. They were a special gift to herself last summer. They are great sandals. I sometimes sneak them on, but I've never worn them outside the house.

"Okay," I say, silently really thankful that I had that recent growth spurt and my mom and I now have the same size feet.

First time I've been happy that I grew so much. I sit on the bed for a long time, looking at my reflection, just hugging my new shirt.

Who is that girl in the mirror, anyhow?

TWENTY-FOUR

It takes a while for me to get ready. I try on too many pairs of pants and leggings with the new green shirt. I try on so many that I actually work up a sweat, but I finally decide that I should wear the newish black leggings I got at Christmas. I put on some deodorant (which is the newest thing I own) and pull on the green shirt.

I brush my hair out straight, which is tricky because when there's even a breath of humidity it curls in giant waves, so I look like a little kid. Mental note. I'll have to keep bugging Mom for that hair straightener. Now she's given me my shirt, I guess there's room for a new present in time for my birthday.

Ever hopeful.

I slip downstairs quietly and slide my feet into Mom's expensive sandals. I take a peek at myself in the hallway mirror.

I'm not sure what I expect to see, but there's definitely something different about me. I'm certain that I look a lot older and a lot more refined in my green shirt. It's sure not like wearing torn old jeans and beat-up T-shirts, although I have no problem with those most of the time.

At that moment the front door opens and the Chrissies run in, armed with squirt guns. My mom runs in behind them, and before they can get any ideas she grabs the guns off them.

They both stand stock still and stare at me with their mouths open. I swear I can hear their little brains working together to say something smart, but they surprise me and stay quiet.

Christine speaks first. "You look pretty, Gwennie. I like that shirt." My brother just stares at me and finally says, "What happened to *you*?"

It could have been much worse. I actually think they may turn into real human beings one day. I smile at them both. They lose interest pretty fast, though, those two. Once I smile and don't react, they wander away to watch TV. Not reacting is a new trick I've discovered when dealing with them, and it seems to work in my favour every time.

My mom is not so easy to shake, though. She is standing between me and the door for a few moments. She says, "You look really great, Gwen. Be home by ten, get someone to walk you or call if you need me to pick you up. Have fun!"

That's it. I head out the door and into the early evening.

I'm Gwennie Golden. I'm a Night Flyer, and I'm going to my first real party.

TWENTY-FIVE

Parties aren't what I expected.

I walk to Martin's house, and when I get there, Martin doesn't even say hello to me. His mom does, though, like a person who hasn't seen you in a long time then realizes that they completely forgot that you existed. She actually says "Oh!" when she sees me, then continues with a brave face by saying my name really slowly, as it comes to her.

I'm polite, though, and do a little bow, which seems to make her more nervous.

I say "Hi, Mrs. Evells, remember me? I used to play here with Martin every day ... when we were little...." She is looking at me and I can't quite place the look. Is it confusion? Amnesia? Horror? I'm not sure, so eventually I just walk away because there doesn't seem to be anything more I can do for her. I do catch a glimpse of her as she hurries back inside her house. She looks upset for some reason.

I wander around to the backyard. A lot of kids are there when I arrive. Most of my class. Most of the grade nine class. There are a few kids I don't recognize, who must be Martin's friends from out of town, because it's impossible not to know everyone in a small town like ours. Shelley Norman and the other giant grade nine girls all laugh when I walk in, but they might have been laughing at a joke, not exactly at me per se. It might have just been bad timing on my part, to walk in during the punchline of a joke. All the same, Shelley makes sure she gives me a good shove with her shoulder when she walks past me to get to the drinks table a little while later.

Could a fight break out between girls at a party? I'm pretty sure that wouldn't be very ladylike, but I really doubt that Shelley cares at all about that.

Noted: avoid Shelley Norman.

After that, I mostly stand around and watch the boys try to get up the nerve to ask the girls to dance.

Jeffrey Parks is there and gives me a wide berth. Sparrow Andrews, another boy from my class, comes up to me. His first name isn't Sparrow, of course, it's David, but Sparrow is a nickname that kind of exactly describes his scrawny build. He comes up to me and, like a little sparrow, hops around in front of me on one foot in the dirt of Martin's backyard. I'm holding a cola at the time. He hops until he bangs into me, and my cola goes all over my new shirt.

"Gosh, m'awful sorry, Gwennie. Djuwanna dance?"

He helps to mop the drink off my shirt, but somehow I just don't have the inclination to dance with him after that. I sure hope my mom can wash the mess out. A few girls come up to me and ask where Jez is. It's a universal truth that my best friend is a lot more popular than me. I shrug, "Barbecue," I say a few times, as casually as I can. I keep looking around for Martin, but I can't find him.

The truth is, I find the strangeness of the event truly mesmerizing. I stand off to one side of the yard, a yard that I have intimate knowledge of, by the way. I ran around in the kiddie pool, floundered through the sprinkler, hid in the hedges, played in the garden playhouse, found secret spots in my little kid world, in that backyard. True, I haven't been here for a while, the trees and bushes are a little bigger maybe, but it is still the backyard of my little kid life. It's mine in a way that it isn't anyone else's.

The fence is covered by pretty lights, and the big tree has a spotlight nailed to it. Martin's parents set up a picnic table with food and drinks, and there is a portable stereo playing music nearby.

Kids are dancing in the spotlight. It's a slow dance, and I'm watching and kind of swaying along with the music, when I feel someone behind me.

I turn around and it's Martin. He smiles his crooked smile and says, "Sorry I didn't say hi before, Gwennie, my mom made me change my shirt. I spilled cola on it."

I laugh and tell him "Yeah, me too."

We both laugh, just like old times.

Then Martin Evells asks me to dance.

Dancing with a boy three inches shorter than you is a little awkward, I have to admit. You really have no choice but to breathe all over his face, and pretty much directly into his nose. You can only hope that your tooth-brushing from several hours before is still holding up.

Still, the niceness is there. Martin is nice. There's just no other word to describe him. Even all these years later, he still smells like lemons. His mom either *really* loves lemon-scented laundry detergent, or that's just Martin's natural smell.

Either way, it's a good smell. We dance a little in the spotlight, and I'm pretty sure I see a few girls look angrily in my general direction. Mrs. Evells even pops her head out the back door a few times to watch us. I get the feeling she wants to say something, but she doesn't.

I don't care.

I'm Gwennie Golden, I'm a Night Flyer, and I'm dancing with a boy. My favourite boy of all time. Martin Evells.

Ten o'clock rolls around before I even know it.

TWENTY-SIX

I will wish I left five minutes earlier than I did. Because what happens next is a little disturbing. I'm not going to sugarcoat it, though. So here it is:

Martin's mom comes out of the house at ten o'clock and says okay everyone, time to leave. She makes a special of note of saying "Gwendolyn Golden, it's time to go," which seems a little unnecessary. I get it. Party's over.

We all say thank you and we head toward the front sidewalk to go home.

All except for me, that is, because Martin won't let me. Once his mom goes back into the house, he sneaks out to the front sidewalk, where I'm aiming to depart, and grabs me. He makes a "shhh" sign with his finger, and we tiptoe back into his yard. It looks desolate and woeful now all the partiers are gone. Dropped napkins and potato chips and half-empty soda cans litter the yard in the dark.

He takes me to the back of the yard, where there's this little garden playhouse. It's all white, with cut-out windows and pretend flower boxes and a wraparound porch. It has a tiny polka-dotted red door with a big green handle. It was a lot of fun once, when we were six. No one our age would go near it now, though. Not something that's so obviously meant for little kids. Which explains why I'm so confused when Martin drags me back there and puts his finger to his lips. "Shhh," he whispers again.

"What are we doing here?" I whisper back, but he doesn't answer me. He just creaks open the little polka-dotted door and leads me into the dark interior of the overgrown dollhouse. In the distance, I can hear all the partygoers slowly leave, saying goodbye to each other.

"Shouldn't you be saying goodbye to everyone?" I ask.

He shakes his head and pushes me inside the playhouse.

"You could fix up the place," I say, looking around. I'm trying to be funny, but the truth is that the little house and the dirt floor and everyone else leaving in the distance starts to make me feel kind of strange. The little house still smells like wood and mice and old paint, just like it did when I was six. I have a sudden rush of little-kid want. I want a popsicle. I want my dolly. I want to go home and take a nap.

Then it dawns on me. There is something slightly wrong with this scenario. It's not what I was expecting from Martin Evells. What did he think we were going to do in here? Play house like we did when we were little?

It doesn't take long for me to get the picture. Clearly Martin *does* want to play house, but it's a grown-up version we definitely never played before.

Before I know what's happening, Martin jumps on me and starts rolling around on top of me in the dirt. He's trying to kiss me, pulling at my hair and grabbing my green shirt. One of my pearl buttons pops off and rolls away. How much damage can my new shirt take? First spilled cola, now this.

I'm starting to get mad.

Now you might think I'd be afraid, but honestly I'm not. First of all, I think I mentioned I'm a good three inches taller than Martin, and much heavier. He hasn't had his growth spurt yet, and I'm most of the way through mine. By the time he starts growing and I stop he'll end up a lot taller than me, but right now, right here in this particular predicament, I definitely have the upper hand.

So I have no choice. I smack that boy hard. I give him a full-barrelled wallop right upside his head, and I make good contact, too.

He grunts in surprise, and says, "Jeez, Gwen, what's the matter with you?"

I say "What's the matter with *you*, Martin? Is this how you treat your guests?"

I get up to leave, and he swears. I push him on his behind and storm out of that playhouse. That's one childhood sanctuary ruined forever, thank you very much, stupid Martin Evells. I'll never remember all those innocent afternoons playing in that house the same way ever again.

I stomp off across his backyard. I can hear him picking himself up in the little house and he starts chasing after me across the grass. I pick it up a little and am just about at the back gate. Everyone is gone now, and the house is dark except for the kitchen light, which is on.

As I put my hand on the latch, he grabs my arm. He isn't too gentle, either.

I snatch my arm back and get ready to plough him another one, even harder this time. I'm getting really angry, now, angrier than I've ever been in my life.

"I swear, Martin, you touch me again and I'm going to hit you into tomorrow," I snarl.

"Sorry, Gwen. Honest, I thought … I thought you liked me?" he says, kind of embarrassed.

I start to create an answer to this, something along the lines of, "Well, that's beside the point here. You don't just jump on a girl no matter how she feels about you," but I never really get the chance. With all that surprise and anger building up inside me, I kind of lose control.

I realize as I'm shouting into his face that his look of surprise is rapidly changing into a worried look, which then pretty much turns into a look of all-out terror. He's staring straight up at me with his mouth open.

I'm shouting down at Martin Evells, because I'm floating off the ground, just above his head.

Clearly this isn't ideal. The situation gets away from me a little, and it isn't exactly what I hoped for at my first party. But there isn't much I can do about it now.

I look down at him right in his very astonished eyes, and I say as calmly as I can, "Next time you try to kiss a girl, stupid, you better ask her first!"

He nods and whimpers, and then he just runs right into his house as fast as he can. The door slams behind him and I even hear him bolt the lock.

What did he think I was going to do, fly into the house yelling at him some more? The thought does occur to me, but I decide against it.

I could fly up to his bedroom and yell at him through the window. But nothing would give me as much pleasure as that first look of terror on his face, so I don't do anything. Besides, it's getting late.

That'll teach him some manners. I'm pretty far off on the whole "Martin Evells-being-so-nice" thing. I'm starting to think that the life-long lemon scent he gave off must just have been all the sourness in him coming out, all along.

TWENTY-SEVEN

I fly home.

I think, *Why not, no one's around. It's getting late. Mom's going to worry.*

There are some handy things about being a Night Flyer, there's no denying it.

I land on the front lawn and crash into the bushes. The door opens immediately and my mom looks out at me. I spit dirt and bushes out of my mouth.

"You're twenty minutes late!" she says.

"Sorry, Mom, I know. I got caught up with Martin," I say, trying not to look her in the eye.

"If you're going to be late again, call me. I was worried silly." She really does look worried.

"You could get me a cellphone," I say helpfully. I've been asking for one for ages, but there's no money for something like that. My mom doesn't bite and just stands at the door looking at me.

"Your shirt is missing a button," is what she finally says.

"Yeah, it has cola on it too. Sparrow Andrews did his sparrow dance in the dirt and then got all excited and spilled my drink on me." My mom looks a little like she wants to laugh, but she doesn't.

"Okay, go in and get changed. I think I can fix it. There's another button inside the seam. Oh, Jez called. She said to call her when you got in."

I breeze into the house past my mom and run up to my room. I tiptoe past the Chrissies' bedroom (they are fast asleep), but peek in. They're kind of cute when they're sleeping. Cassie is curled up on their floor, snoring. Their lives haven't been interrupted by blazing hormones or flying jags or crazed teenagers trying to kiss them. For a moment I have a yearning, strong as anything: it would be nice to be seven years old again, it really would.

My room is quiet and dark, which is good because I need some time to think.

A boy was once my best friend, when we were six. We played together all the time. Then we stopped. I still really like him and I've known him forever. He is also a giant jerk and made me really mad. When I got mad, I lost control and flew. When I flew, I yelled in his face.

It sure taught him a lesson. But it's clearly not ideal. I would like to have a little more self-control.

I get into my pyjamas, reach under my bed, and lift the brochure from the handbook. I look down the list of questions:

#4: How do I control my flying?

As noted in Question #2 (What is a Night Flyer?), Night Flying, or the ability to fly, usually begins during puberty, although sometimes much later, and except in a few very rare cases, almost never before. Since puberty is a time of great hormonal flux, you may find that you fly when you least want to, such as at times of stress, anger, sudden upset, or joy. Sometimes you may fly simply during a moment of boredom or carelessness. Young Night Flyers generally outgrow this troubling problem quickly. With practice, focus on breathing techniques, and the help of your Mentor, most Flyers gain increasing control of their flight patterns within a few days or weeks of their First Flight.

Despite reminding me a little too much of an uncomfortable sex education class we had to take in grade seven, this answer is pretty straightforward, but not entirely reassuring.

I wonder what happens to Night Flyers who have a terrible temper, like mine? The brochure says, "*most* Flyers gain increasing control."

Does that mean me?

I'm reading the next entry, *#2: What is a Night Flyer,* which tells me pretty much what I was expecting: *A Night Flyer is anyone (although most often a young teenager or adolescent entering puberty) who has taken his or her First Flight. The First Flight usually occurs in a*

safe and controlled manner with the young Night Flyer's
parents, Watcher, and Mentor cheering him or her on ...

... when the phone rings. It's Jez. Her voice is
all low and breathy, like her mom is asleep and she
doesn't want her to hear.

"So," she breathes. "How was it? How was
Martin's party?" She's never mad at me, not even
for not calling her when I say I will. This is one of
the main reasons that she's always going to be my
best friend.

I put the brochure and handbook away under
my bed in case my mom walks in, then I tell her
everything. About how pretty the backyard looked,
and who was there. She wouldn't let me get off easy
on that either. I had to recite the names of every
single person I could remember, and my memory
isn't that good.

Finally, though, I get to the end and then I
tell her about what happened with Martin in the
playhouse, and the part after.

Her voice gets that worried edge to it. "You *flew*
in front of him?"

"Yeah, so what?" I say. Is there something I'm
missing?

"Well, Gwen, what if he *tells* someone?"

Oh, no. That just didn't occur to me. What if
stupid Martin-lemony-Evells decides to open his big
yap and tell the whole world about me?

My secret would be out.

"Uh-oh. I didn't think about that. What am I
going to do?" I start to sweat.

I get up and open my bedroom window, where a little breeze is making the trees outside dance around. Funny how that doesn't intrigue me at all tonight, when last night it was about the only thing my body cared for in the whole world.

"Wait, let me think," she says. I swear I can hear her thinking. It's a giant, raspy, grinding sound.

Okay, that's mean. Jez is plenty smart. I let her noisy-thinking brain work for a minute, but my own brain is working out something faster.

I say, "You know, no one is going to believe him."

"What do you mean?"

"I mean, even if he tells someone that I yelled at him while I was flying around above his head, who would believe him?"

I can hear her nodding. "Maybe ..." she says.

"No, really, Jez. Think about it. It's not the movies. I'm not a superhero or something, I'm just ... me. And besides, I can tell you he was *really* scared."

"Maybe you're right, Gwen. But I don't know." She doesn't sound convinced.

But I am. I know I'm right. Stupid Martin isn't going to tell anyone. He's a scared baby who runs for cover when you yell at him. I bet even if you aren't yelling at him in the air above his head.

Although that might have given me the edge, just a little.

TWENTY-EIGHT

I hang up with Jez, then toss and turn a bit.

When I finally fall asleep, I sleep like crazy. I just sleep and sleep and sleep. I don't remember any dreams, though. I think that maybe my waking life is becoming so interesting that I don't need to dream things up anymore.

I sleep in until noon. The house is quiet when I wake up, so Mom must have taken the Chrissies to the park or something. I drag myself around my room, banging into things until I wake up enough to realize I'm not actually touching the ground.

So I think really hard about touching down onto my carpeted floor, and my body slowly obeys me, but not willingly or anything. It feels a little like a Battle of Wills, the kind that Mom sometimes has when she wants the Chrissies to do something they aren't so keen on.

What am I going to do today? I'm going to take a few minutes to finish reading the brochure. I'm also going to go over to The Float Boat as soon as decently possible, to see if Mrs. Forest is back yet.

But first, I should eat. Yes, definitely, I'll start with that.

I throw some frozen waffles into the toaster and pull some blueberry jam out of the fridge. Something's gnawing at me, though.

What if Jez is right? What if Martin *does* tell people what happened last night?

My flying is private. It's my secret, and I want to keep it that way.

What will I be willing to do to protect it? This question worries me all morning and keeps me from getting much done.

I can't barge in on Mrs. Forest yet, since it's Sunday. So I go and sit on my bed for a while and read the rest of the brochure. The most important entries as far as I see them are frustratingly short and unhelpful:

#3: Is Night Flying Dangerous?
Generally, no. Ask your Mentor for further instruction.

#9: Can I lead a normal life?
Generally, yes. Ask your Mentor for further instruction.

And my favourite:

#10: How many Night Flyers are there?
The Night Flyer population rises and falls, each day.

For a moment, I curse my Less-than-Willing status. I just *know* that the More-than-Willing get a lot more information than this in the full edition of the handbook. And the word "generally" can allow for pretty wild exceptions, at least in my experience with the word.

I'm getting annoyed, so I put the brochure away and go out to play catch with the Chrissies when they come back from the park. I walk Cassie around the neighbourhood before dinner. I walk along the main street near The Float Boat, but the doors are locked and there's a CLOSED sign in the window. I sincerely want to talk to Mrs. Forest, but there's no one around. She and Mr. Forest live above the store, but I just can't see ringing the doorbell. It's not an emergency or anything, and I don't even know if Mrs. Forest is back from visiting her sister.

I walk on. The streets are deserted, until …

… I hear a bicycle turn the nearest corner.

It's Martin.

He looks straight at me and then he seems petrified. He screeches on his brakes and we have no choice but to stare at each other for a second.

I cringe inside, just a little.

Cassie, bless her doggie heart, wags her tail at seeing him. I guess she remembers him from all those little kid play dates.

He makes up his mind and starts pedalling as fast as he can. He has no choice but to ride right past me. He whizzes by on his bike and yells at me, "Just don't come near me, Gwennie, ya hear!" He puts his head down and pedals like he's being chased by a hellhound. Cassie starts to bark like she's going to chase him. *That* I'd like to see!

My mind is hesitating, but my body seems pretty fired up. I tear out of my shoes and sprint barefoot along the sidewalk, dragging Cassie with me. She's so slow that I drop her leash, and that's when I really start running.

I catch up to his bike and I shout, "You tell anyone about last night, and I swear, Martin Evells, I'll fly outside your window singing opera at the top of my lungs every night for the rest of your life!" Okay, so it's come to this. I'm going to terrorize someone into shutting up. Am I being a bully? Or am I just taking care of myself?

He stops. He actually screeches on his brakes and turns to stare at me. There is a horrified look on his face again, but it's mixed with something else. A tiny hint of sadness. Or concern. Or maybe I just don't know him very well and that's how he looks when he hates someone.

Martin's mouth makes a very surprised looking "oh" and his dark eyes get even wider. That boy looks like he could burst into tears. But he doesn't. Instead he just shakes his head a little, and I hear him whisper, "*Jeez*, Gwennie!"

We look at each other. There's a long moment of looking that could have ended differently maybe, if we were older. But we don't know what to say, and we're scared.

The moment leaves us. So he puts his head down once more and pedals as fast as he can away from me. I hear him shout over his quickly receding shoulder, "You just keep clear of me, Gwennie Golden!" but his voice quavers, and he sounds like a scared little kid.

Not the exact effect I want to have on boys, but maybe this is the new me?

TWENTY-NINE

After seeing Martin on the street, I walk Cassie home really slowly. I drag my sorry feet and even Cassie seems impatient with me.

I don't hear from Mrs. Forest, so I can only guess that she isn't back yet. The night is very ordinary. I have dinner. I help Mom get my brother and sister to bed. I do some homework. I phone Jez.

But what is most ordinary is that I sleep.

I just sleep. I go to sleep, and I wake up in the morning and I'm not on the ceiling. And I don't wake up bumping into my window at any time during the night, with my crazy body trying to escape into the outside world.

No. I wake up like everyone else, in my bed. Suddenly I almost miss the thrill of waking up in the wrong place, up instead of down.

School is ordinary, too. No flutters, no random hovering body parts, no mad dashes into the staff washroom. No Martin sightings either, which is probably just as well. I hear from Jez later on that he didn't come to school today.

It's almost dull, being so ordinary.

After school, though, I make a special trip to The Float Boat to see Mrs. Forest. She still isn't back from visiting her sister, which upsets me.

While the Chrissies are squealing around the store (it is Monday after all, we never go to The Float Boat except on Fridays after school, so I can see why they are pretty excited), I kind of corner Mr. Forest.

He's standing by himself beside the float machine, looking through a newspaper spread out on the counter. There's no one else in the store at this particular moment.

"Mr. Forest?" I say.

He looks up from his paper and smiles. "Why, Ms. Gwendolyn Golden, what can I do for you?"

I shuffle my feet a little. I'm not really sure how to start this conversation.

"Well, Mr. Forest, I'm just thinking that maybe you know a thing or two about …" I drop my voice and look over at my brother and sister, who are too far gone into the jelly bean wall to notice me.

"… a thing or two about Night Flyers," I finish. My voice is so low, though, I'm not sure he hears me.

Oh, but he does hear me. I look into his face and I see the kindest, deepest look in his eyes that I've ever seen on anybody. He just nods and smiles a little.

"Well, Gwennie, I thought you might ask me sometime. Just a minute." He takes two empty candy bags from the shelf, walks over to the Chrissies and says, "Christine. Christopher. Today isn't your birthday, is it, by any chance?"

The twins stop and stare. Christine, who is just a tad quicker on the uptake than our brother, sizes up the situation and flashes a really winning smile at Mr. Forest. She says, "No, it's not Mr. Forest, but we just had it!"

He smiles and nods, hands them each a candy bag, and says, "Okay then, let's pretend it *is* your birthday. Go have fun!"

The twins become an unstoppable squealing, whirling ball with four blazing arms and two spinning heads, gearing up to top speed. They are going to explode before they fill those bags with free candy. And they are *loud*.

Mr. Forest takes me by the arm and says, "Let's just step outside, should we?"

"Good idea," I say. There really isn't any choice with those two in their current jelly bean frenzy.

We step out onto the wooden porch surrounding the store, and we sit in an old rocking swing. Mr. Forest swings us a little and looks at me.

"Well, Gwen, I hear you and Mrs. Forest had a good time the other night?"

"I'm not sure how good it was, Mr. Forest. It was interesting, though. It's just that I have so many questions, and Mrs. Forest isn't here and I'm kind of ready to burst not knowing some things."

"Okay, Gwen, most of the answers should be in the handbook, but ask away. I'll answer whatever I can."

"Well, actually, I didn't get the whole handbook," I say, looking away from him. Suddenly I'm feeling stupid, like the stupidest kid in the world. Too stupid for the big kid handbook.

Mr. Forest scratches his head. "You didn't?" he asks, confused.

"Well, there isn't really any book to read, it's kind of just empty, like a box. I got a three-page brochure instead, with ten questions and answers," I say, suddenly miserable.

"Oh, I see," he says. He sounds surprised. He's not familiar with stupid kids like me, maybe.

"It's just a letter, a brochure, and a feather in there. It's a fake book," I continue. I'm mad now. I cross my arms.

"Gwen, you just get what you need. Everyone's handbook is different. That's how it is, you understand?"

I nod. This is a relief, I guess, to know that I might not be the only Less-than-Willing Reader out there, not the only person to get the handbook -lite version.

"But I have questions the brochure doesn't answer. Like, what's the Flight Crew, Local 749?"

Mr. Forest laughs out loud. "Oh Gwen, that's a joke! There's not really any Flight Crew 749 exactly. The handbook comes from your Mentor, Mrs. Forest. That's just her joke. She and Mr. McGillies are what she calls your Flight Crew. That's the street address of The Float Boat, 749." He swings us a little as he chuckles.

How did I not make the connection that 749 is the street number of the only candy store in town? I look up a little, and there are the numbers, 7-4-9, big and brassy, right beside the front door of The Float Boat.

I've spent my entire childhood looking at those numbers every time I walk into the store. How could I not think of that? I really don't pay enough attention to the world around me.

There's a silence for a bit. I can hear the Chrissies spinning around in the store, getting louder and louder. I have to press on here; I need answers. I'm waiting for something to crash to the ground inside the store, then I'll lose Mr. Forest for good.

"Are you a Night Flyer, too?" I ask.

He shakes his head. "Nope, never was. Not so much as a flutter."

I nod. Okay, so it's just Mrs. Forest. And apparently flyers and non-flyers can meet up and live long, happy lives together, just like question nine in the brochure said. So I'm not doomed to a lifetime of freakish solitude or anything.

"Is there anyone else who can fly like me and Mrs. Forest?" I ask. That question ten was altogether too vague for my liking.

He leans his head to one side. "Well, yes and no. There are more people who can fly, but not in our little town. There was another one, but he's gone now." Mr. Forest looks at me a long time. Then he says, "As far as we know, it's just you two for now, anyway."

"What do you mean, 'for now'?"

"Well, people are born all the time, Gwen. You never know when another flyer is going to come into the world. Or when they're going to leave it." This last part he says very softly.

Just what the brochure said for question ten. He seems a little sad, so I change the subject.

"How many Night Flyers are there, do you think?"

He whistles and pushes back in the swing. "Not many, Gwen. You're pretty special. But we knew that, didn't we?" He's trying to be funny, but I don't have time for funny.

"Yeah, but how many?" I persist. I really need to know.

"Not a lot. Maybe a dozen in all this part of the country. Like I say, you're a rare and special breed, you and Mrs. Forest."

I'm just going to ask how he knows there are a dozen Night Flyers in our part of the country when the big crash I was waiting for inside the store happens. Mr. Forest flinches but doesn't hurry to get in there. I guess a lifetime of working in a store with excited children eating sugary treats can make you unusually calm. Either that or you'd die young.

He stands and says, "I got one more thing to say, Gwen: just don't let anyone take it away from you. You may hear from different places that you can't really fly, or that you shouldn't be flying. That it's bizarre, or wrong. Don't listen. This is your special gift, not anyone else's. Only you can choose."

I'm not really sure what he means, but I nod like I do.

My special gift.

Why couldn't my special gift be making banana bread, or playing soccer, or being great at chess or something?

My special gift is just too strange.

THIRTY

I take my brother and sister home, and it ends up being a pretty ordinary night. I help my mom make dinner, but I tell her I have too much homework to help her get C2 to bed, and she lets me escape to my room.

It's been four days since I learned I could fly. It's been two days since I've flown, properly. I decide that there's just no way I'm not going to go out and fly tonight, with or without Mrs. Forest. I'm dying to get out into the night breeze and feel the wind on my face, but I'm a little scared to do it alone.

I call Jez, and I tell her I need to see her, and I want to meet in the park. There is a little park exactly halfway between our two houses, and we have always met there when we need to talk. We even sneak out at night sometimes in the summer to meet, but it's a little risky. It's not something we do all the time or anything.

She agrees to meet me in an hour. I wait in my room, and Cassie curls up with me, licking my face. I turn out my lights and say goodnight when my mom comes to check on me. I even have a pair of pyjamas on over my real clothes, so she won't get suspicious. The house gets quiet, and I know the Chrissies are asleep. Cassie falls asleep on my bed, and my mother turns her light out in her room.

Somewhere around eleven thirty, I take off my fake pyjamas, tiptoe across my bedroom, and open my window. The moonlight falls onto the Night Flyer's handbook half hidden under my bed, and I feel a stirring of guilt. Mrs. Forest said not to go out alone, but I can't stop myself.

I have to go out and fly tonight or I feel like I'm going to die.

I undo the hook and open the screen. It's wide open out there. Cassie stirs a little on my bed, but she doesn't wake up.

I'm standing kind of halfway balanced on the window ledge. This suddenly isn't like the other night with all the desire in the world pushing me out the window, overriding every good thought in my head. This is more like thinking. I sit on the window ledge and close my eyes. I'm not sure I can do this.

But Jez is waiting.

I breathe in deep. I smell moisture in the good soil working away, about to do its best to grow rows and rows of corn in the fields all around town. I smell flowers close by, giving off their scent for no good reason other than to be sweet to humans and bees. A warm breeze flutters across my cheek and draws me out of myself, and suddenly I am hovering just outside my bedroom window.

Just like I wanted to.

It's another beautiful night. I'm breathing a little too fast, so I do what Mrs. Forest said, and I slow it down. I think about breathing in and out, really slowly, and concentrate on each breath. I start to walk through the air, in the general direction of the little park a few streets away. Just as I leave my backyard, I hear a familiar voice say quietly, "You be careful up there, missy, you're on your own."

I look over at my neighbour's house, and Mr. McGillies is sitting on the back porch lawn chair, just like he lives there. His shopping cart full of empty bottles is parked nearby in the neighbour's driveway. I frown and can't think what to say. It feels a little like getting caught.

"Don't worry, Mr. McGillies," I finally say. "I'm pretty sure I can do this just fine. I'll be back really soon."

I don't wait for his answer and just keep air-walking toward the meeting place with Jez. It's slow, though. I don't want to air-walk anymore, I want to fly and swoop and zip around like I did that first night.

It takes me a while, but finally I see the little park. Jez is waiting on the picnic bench, where she always waits. I want to surprise her, and if I'm being honest here, I want to impress her as well, so I pick up speed. I start going faster and faster, and I think I can do some cool tricks in the air right in front of Jez, so I swoop really low because I want to do a somersault and land perfectly on my feet.

Instead, I crash straight into the ground, like a rock.

I still can't get the hang of landing.

My head is spinning and I can't see very well because there is blood in my eyes. Jez runs over and kind of squeals when she sees the blood. She gets out a tissue and starts dabbing at me, making these cooing, mothering sounds. I push her away.

"Cut it out, Jez, it's nothing. Just leave me." I'm mad because my great smart-ass landing turned into a crash landing.

"You're hurt," is all she says. I take the tissue and hold it to my forehead. It doesn't hurt much, so I'm not too worried. But Jez is.

"What was so important that we had to sneak out tonight, Gwen? It's not even summer, and we have school tomorrow." She sounds hurt.

"I don't know, I just needed to get out. I'm mad at Martin." Jez makes me tell her again what happened, and she gets mad too, and says all the right things. She says stuff like, "That Martin *is* evil! Remember we used to call him Evil Evells? Well it's true! He's creepy!"

But I tell her that I don't feel so great about finding out that the boy I liked for my entire life is a complete jerk.

How could I be so wrong about someone? It is definitely confusing.

The blood stops dripping down my forehead enough for Jez to take a better look at my cut. She cleans it a little with some water from her water bottle, then says it's fine, just a cut under my hairline. No one will even notice, she says.

We talk for a while, sitting in the swings. She tells me about some of the boy cousins her age, acting all crazy and stealing cars, or breaking windows, or on the lighter side of things forgetting homework or skipping soccer practice.

I say I don't care, Martin's a creep and he should ask before he kisses a girl. Jez agrees and adds that maybe I should just avoid that boy for now. Eventually she says all she has to say and yawns, then gets up to go home.

She's right, I should just ignore that boy. It's really late, so I float alongside Jez until she's home.

"Aren't you tired too?" she asks as she sneaks through the back door into her house.

"No, I'm not. I'm honestly not tired at all."

"G'night, Gwen. See you tomorrow."

Jez shuts the door, locks it, and then I fly up to her bedroom window to make sure she tucks in. She does, and I wave at her through the window. I hear her say, "'Night, Gwen. Jeez, go to bed already, it's two o'clock in the morning."

I know I should, but I'm not going to go to bed.

Not tonight. No way.

THIRTY-ONE

I should listen to Jez. She's smarter than me. I should go home to bed while I have the chance.

But I don't.

Instead I start to float gently around the streets of our little town. I'm about roof height from the ground, and I really feel like nothing can ever hurt me. There's no one around except cats, who don't seem to find it odd that a human is silently zipping along above their heads. One cat scampers on the road below me, looking up at me and meowing now and then. I fly down and hover, and gently scratch its back where it arches up to meet my hand.

I see that cat hiding in the bushes and darting out at night bugs and moths, silently following along below me. It feels comforting to have a sweet shadow like that. The cat and I dart at each other and play tag for a while, it hiding and jumping and batting at me when I fly by, as though I'm a bird. Then, in the way of cats, it whisks its tail and disappears.

I'm alone. The streetlights buzz as I fly past them. I see all the stores and houses that I have known all my life, smaller and boxier, like a toy town, below my feet. When I think of a toy town, I think of Martin's backyard playhouse, and I can't stop it. I get mad.

And suddenly more than anything I want to yell in his bedroom window that he's a jerk and he should be ashamed of himself.

A tiny part of me says that probably isn't a terrific idea, but a much bigger part of me wants to yell at Martin Evells some more. I want to find him in his little boy pyjamas (maybe with trucks on them, like Christopher's), tucked up in his cozy Spiderman sheets, and let him have a serious piece of my mind.

Maybe I *will* start singing opera at the top of my lungs, just like I said.

So I fly over to his house. If I could take it back, I would. I'm not proud of what happens next, but I can't change it. I want to be honest here.

I'm looking in the windows of Martin's house. His house is tall and skinny and surrounded by tall trees, so it takes a while for me to work my way in.

First I peek into his parents' room. Sleeping. Then the bathroom window. Empty. Then the guest room. Also empty.

Then I peek in Martin's window. He is sleeping, of course, since it's about three o'clock in the morning now, but no matter how hard I look, I can't be sure about the truck pyjamas or Spiderman sheets. He's all quiet and happy-looking, though, and a teddy bear is stuck under his arm.

A big boy like that with a teddy bear? I'm not sure why, but there's something about the comfort and happiness of that boy with that bear that just gets to me.

And something inside me starts up, and I get to yelling. And I really can't stop. I start yelling that he's a jerk ...

... and why did he stop being my friend when we were little?

... and why didn't his mother remember who I was?

... and why didn't he call on me to play anymore, right after my father died, right when I really needed a friend but instead he forgot me or something?

The yelling goes on for a while in that general tone.

Then there's a whole sea of sad inside me, waiting to get out, and I can't even tell you what I'm yelling anymore. It's like a pot starts to boil, and I don't know how to stop it.

I should stop when Martin's scared white face presses up against the window on the other side of my yelling. I should stop when I hear him through the glass, pleading, "Quiet, Gwennie! Go home! I mean it, cut it out right now! *Pleeeezzz!*"

I should stop when I see the light in his parents' room click on, and I definitely should stop when Mr. McGillies rumbles by with his cart on the sidewalk below me to tell me the police are coming.

I don't, though. I don't stop. I yell and curse and cry at Martin Evells, filled with sadness and aloneness, until the police turn down the street.

I swear, I could have kept on all night.

THIRTY-TWO

The police car turns into Martin's driveway. The whole Evells family is out on the front porch in their pyjamas, looking scared. I can see them through the trees a little.

I get a feeling that I'm the bad guy, like in those crime shows where the camera is peeking at the good guys through the bushes. My mouth stops shouting but I can't for the life of me stop staring at what's happening on the Evells' front porch.

Mrs. Evells is pointing in my direction and talking to the policeman as he gets out of his car. I can hear her in that faraway whisper that some-times gets too loud. "She's prowling around up there on a ladder or something. She's that crazy girl, Gwendolyn Golden. The one whose father vanished or died or whatever. She's on drugs." I see Martin looking worriedly up in my direction, too. He bites his lip.

The policeman nods politely and looks up, but I fly behind a tree, and he doesn't see me.

Why would she think I'm on drugs? I hate drugs.

Then I remember. She *did* catch me and Jez smoking a cigarette in the alley behind the pharmacy last summer, but we threw it away as soon as we saw her. Some stupid big kids further down the alley were smoking drugs, not us, but I guess she got the wrong idea. We did look pretty guilty. We've never smoked a cigarette since, either, by the way.

My heart starts to pound.

What have I done? How am I going to get out of this? What's wrong with me? I'm acting like a crazy person, a criminal, a nutcase.

That's when a warm voice says, close to my ear, "Gwennie Golden, I think you'd better come with me, don't you?"

I close my eyes. I don't even need to say a word, I just nod and keep my eyes squeezed shut really tight, and Mrs. Forest takes my hand. It's warm and real and I grab it like I'm going to die if I let go. We fly fast and silent, back through the streets toward my home, far away from Martin's house.

Big tears slosh down my face, and I swear I rain a whole cloud onto the streets of my little town as Mrs. Forest and I fly home.

Martin stopped being my friend right after my dad died.

Just when I needed his friendship the most.

That's a hurt I never saw coming, which is humiliating. I've just never made the connection before, Martin and my dad lost at the same time, and I can't stop crying.

For someone who just recently started crying again, I'm sure doing a lot of it.

But it's not enough, I know, to wash away the shame and pain of how I feel. So I just keep crying.

We land together on the soft grass of my front lawn, and I look at Mrs. Forest. I'm confused. Why aren't we going in my bedroom window like last time? She walks me up to my front door, and I'm really shocked when she rings the doorbell.

She looks at me, and I can see that she's sad, too. She lays her big hand on my shoulder and says, "Sorry, Gwen, honey, but your mom's going to have that nice young police officer here any minute. Let's at least get the right words into her head before that happens."

I'm numb. I'm still weeping a little, and tears are kind of streaming down my face without my knowing it. I couldn't stop them even if I had to. I think I have leaves from the trees outside Martin's window in my hair, and suddenly the cut on my forehead from the park really starts to hurt.

I sniffle a little. Mrs. Forest puts her warm arm around me and rings my doorbell again. After a few more rings, my mother appears at the door in her old dressing gown, her face all white and tired and surprised-looking.

She sizes us up pretty quickly, though. My mother is plenty smart. She and Mrs. Forest don't say much to each other, except I hear Mrs. Forest say, "She's alright, Elizabeth, just a little scared," and I hear my mother say back, "Thank you, Emmeline."

I've almost never heard Mrs. Forest and my mom speak to each other before, except politely at The Float Boat, or over the ice cream stall at the occasional town picnic. I didn't know they were on a first-name basis. It's like they kind of immediately understand something, and Mrs. Forest hands me off to my mom, who puts her arm around me and sweeps me into the house. I hear Mrs. Forest say, "I'll put the coffee on. They'll be here any minute."

Almost like they really aren't all that surprised. Almost like they were both expecting this.

I have to be honest, I kind of blank out from here on. My mother takes me to my bedroom and helps me get into some pyjamas. I'm not talking, and my mother doesn't say anything either, but I don't get the feeling that she's mad at me. She seems a little preoccupied, actually.

She pats my hair as I lay on my pillow and she says to go to sleep. Soon I smell delicious coffee coming from downstairs, and I hear the doorbell ring, and I hear Mrs. Forest's voice mix pleasantly with a man's voice.

I drift off to sleep, and still my mother sits on the edge of my bed a long while, and I have a sense that she is sitting there forever. But I also know that at one point during the night, she gets up and goes to my window and swings open the screen. I peek and there she is with her elbows propped on the window ledge, looking up into the night sky.

She must have gone to speak to the police officer at some point. She must have gone to bed eventually, unless she and Mrs. Forest stayed up all night talking.

But I have no memory or proof of that.

All I remember before I fall asleep is the moonlight shining on my mother's beautiful hair, and that her face is full of tears.

THIRTY-THREE

I wake up late. Someone has closed my screen, but not the blinds, and the sun is streaming onto my face. Cassie is looking at me and wriggles her stubby tail a little when I open my eyes.

She looks expectant. She needs to pee.

Which means that Mom and the twins are out. I'm groggy and tired. I feel really weird and shake my head and generally take too long to get moving. I sit up in bed and run my hands through my hair.

It's Tuesday morning, isn't it? Shouldn't I be at school? Why didn't Mom wake me up?

Then I remember everything that happened last night. It's kind of like remembering a bad dream, then remembering that it isn't a dream, that it's real. Then wondering what on earth is going to happen to you.

I must be in huge trouble, possibly with *the law*, for waking up Martin's family like a screaming lunatic at three o'clock in the morning.

I vaguely remember Mrs. Evells saying something to a police officer about me being on drugs.

But more importantly, what, exactly, did Martin's family see? Did the police officer and Martin's family see me shrieking around the sky like a bat from hell?

Do they know I can fly?

I go downstairs and there is a note for me on the kitchen table. It is in my mother's big, scrawling handwriting. It says: *Gwen, stay home until I come back. We'll talk. Soup on the stove. Luv Mom xx*

There is another little note beside it, in really neat handwriting, which says: *Gwennie, I'm sorry I was away for so long. Come talk to me as soon as you can. E. Forest*

There's also a yellow and black ticket, like a parking ticket, sitting beside both notes. It must be from the police officer's notebook. I don't really want to look at that one, but there's no way I can't. I take a peek:

Violation, Town of Bass Creek
Presiding Officer: Scott B. Taunton
Youth: Gwendolyn Imogen Golden
Age: 13 yrs
Sex: Female
Charge/Noted: Unchaperoned Minor. Disorderly Conduct in Public
Further Notes: parent/s strongly cautioned, first violation

As I take this in, I hear Cassie whining and licking her lips at the back door. I open it for her, and she runs outside and squats to pee as soon as she hits the grass. The look of relief on that dog's face is almost laughable.

But I can't laugh. *Unchaperoned Minor. Disorderly Conduct in Public.*

Parent/s strongly cautioned.

First violation.

I sit at the table and stare some more at the police officer's note. I'm written up in a policeman's book. They've started a file on me somewhere. They know my middle name.

I'm in trouble with *the law*. Worse than that though, possibly many, many people are going to know that I *can fly*.

I lay my head on the kitchen table and look sideways out the glass back door. Cassie's doggie face is now begging me to let her come back in. But I can't muster up the energy to move. I may just lie here on the table all day.

But I don't get to stay here too long. I hear my mom come in and put her keys on the front desk, and there she is in the kitchen, a bag of groceries under her arm, just like it's another normal day.

Not like her eldest child had a recent run-in with the law. Not like her daughter is suddenly the town criminal. Possibly soon to be a jailbird. One that can fly.

I sit up and look at her, and I don't say anything. My mom sits down at the table and takes my hands, and the next words out of her mouth are like a slow-motion video that I'll remember until the day I die:

"Gwen, I'm sorry. I didn't know that it would ever matter to anyone else but me ... but now I know I should have told you. See the thing is ... your dad ... well, he was a Night Flyer, just like you."

And I couldn't have been more surprised than if she told me I was born on a different planet, and my real parents were aliens with spiky green skin.

THIRTY-FOUR

But it does explain a lot.

I must look very confused. And mad.

Mom and I rarely talk about Dad anymore. We both think about him, I know that. At Christmas, and on his birthday, and a few weeks before the twins' birthday each year, we kind of both sniffle more than usual. When I was little, Mom would take out a photo album of Dad, and we'd look at it together at those times of year. More and more lately, though, she takes it out and looks at it alone, and leaves it around for me to look at.

But mostly I don't, and the photo album disappears again after a few days.

My mom says again, "I know you're a Night Flyer, Gwen. Emmeline Forest told me last night. I should have guessed, but I didn't know it was something you could pass on to your kids. Usually it's both parents who can fly ... then the children, yes, maybe ... but it was just your dad ... and your grandparents died before you were born, so I couldn't check with them, and your dad didn't know either. No one knew."

I get a really stern look on my face and cross my arms. I nod a little.

I skip the whole so-you-can-fly-and-oh-by-the-way-your-dad-could-fly-too phase of this conversation, and get to the important stuff.

"Am I in trouble?" I ask.

My mom shakes her head. "No. You mean about last night? No. I don't know exactly what Emmeline said to that young police officer, but we got off with a warning. This time."

I have a sudden clear image of Police Officer Scott B. Taunton standing in Martin's driveway, looking up into the trees for me. He's young, almost boyish, for a police officer. Perhaps he ate a lot of candy when he was a kid, or really liked floats.

I have a hunch he is no stranger to The Float Boat, though, and probably owes Mrs. Forest a favour or two.

"You should know something else, though," my mother continues in a voice that says she really doesn't want to go on with the next sentence.

"You should know that Mrs. Evells phoned me and told me this morning that you are in *no way* to contact her son again. Ever."

There's a long pause, and I look out the kitchen window. I know my mom wants me to say something, but I just can't. I can't look at her. I can't mention Martin. I'm not talking about Dad.

"I'm sorry, Gwen," Mom says gently, in an "I-understand-how-you-feel" tone. But I'm not tackling that topic. I'm not talking about my feelings right now. I'm just not.

"Okay, I'm not in trouble. Why didn't you wake me up to go to school then?" I ask instead. My mom looks uncomfortable and kind of hems and haws a little.

"Honestly, Gwen, I think it might be better if you don't go back to school. It's over next week anyway, and I already talked to Janet Abernathy. She's fine with you taking the rest of the school year off. But it's up to you."

So my mother talked to my principal and I'm not supposed to go back to school? I look into her face. She seems tired. And worried, maybe.

But I'm mad, and I hang onto it. I think about the secret my mom has kept about my dad all these years. I think about that flimsy three-page brochure up in my handbook, and I think about not going to school to finish grade eight, like any normal kid.

"I *can* go to school, though, if I want to, right?" I ask sharply.

"Yes, you can," my mother says quietly. "But I thought it might be easier for you not to see, well, not to have to bump into Martin in the hallways. It might be kind of awkward for both of you. Plus you might want to take a little time for yourself, Gwen, to figure out what's going on ... how it feels to be a, you know ... flyer person."

I stand up and say something that amazes even me, because I've never thought too hard about this kind of thing before. But I say, "No, Mom, I have to go back to school. I'll keep clear of Martin. But I want to go. I have to hold my head up. And as for flying, I'll figure it out. Besides, I have Mrs. Forest to help me."

That last sentence is mean-spirited, and I know it. My mom can't help it that she's not a flyer, that she can't guide me in this flying thing at all. Dad could have. But he's not here. Mrs. Forest is.

But my mom doesn't react to my meanness. She nods. She says okay, I can go back to school. She tells me she loves me and we can talk more about Dad, about everything, but she has one request right now.

She says, "Gwennie, promise me you won't go flying again until school is over?" I nod and promise.

"And one more thing," she says. "Promise me you'll never, *never* fly alone at night again? Let me or Mrs. Forest know if you're going … okay?"

She says this in a voice that sounds like she really means it. It scares me a little.

I nod.

"What about Mr. McGillies?" I ask. My mom looks at me like she has no idea what I'm talking about.

So I say, "Should I let Mr. McGillies know I'm going flying, too?"

She says, "You mean the old bottle man with the cart?"

"Yeah," I answer, a little surprised that he doesn't figure as large in her life as he does in mine. She gets thoughtful and puts her head on one side. I can see she's thinking a lot of things, but I don't know what.

"Can he fly, too?" she finally asks.

"No."

"I guess if he's the only one around, then, yes. Better to tell him than no one."

Suddenly I understand something. My mother has no idea that other people have been looking out for me my whole life. That even without Dad around, there are people keeping an eye on me.

That she's not alone.

THIRTY-FIVE

The next day I go to school. I sit in class, and I don't fly. I don't see Martin Evells, although there is a near-sighting in the lunchroom. Martin is with Jeffrey Parks and Sparrow Andrews and a bunch of other boys, most of them staring and whispering. Martin looks at me, though, not whispering and pointing. He looks a little sad. When I turn to look at them, they all run off, him included. Not exactly the reaction I want from all the boys in school.

Other than Martin's friends, most kids are paying me about the regular amount of attention, meaning they ignore me. People aren't pointing and staring like I'm a full-blown crazy person, so I guess Martin either kept his mouth shut or hasn't had time to tell everyone about what happened after the party.

Or that I was shouting in his window at three o'clock in the morning, doing a pretty good impression of a crazy person.

Nope, no one seems to suspect a thing. So at least for now, I'm still just plain old Gwennie Golden to everyone.

So I take the last few days of school, and I survive them. I sit with Jez at lunch, or my little brother and sister, and kind of just hang out. I'm too preoccupied to care much about what is going on at school anyway. At home, Mom keeps starting conversations with me, about flying, about Dad, about what life holds for me in the years to come, but we keep getting interrupted by C2 and eventually I can see that she's happy to just let it slide.

But it's okay, I don't really want that conversation anyway. The future really doesn't interest me all that much. The present day is taking up pretty much all my waking energy as it is.

I keep my promise to her, and I don't fly again during school. It's hard, though. For a few nights I just sleep, but on the second last night of school, I want out of my room in the worst way. I start to imagine what it's like to be an animal in a trap, and I pace around my room. The warm early summer night is calling me outside. The trees and the grass smell terrific, the leaves are whispering in the breeze, "Come on out, Gwennie!"

But I don't. Instead, I slam my window shut, roar downstairs, and stay up all night on the couch watching old TV reruns.

When I wake up, it's the last day of school, and I'm covered in a blanket, which Mom must have put on me. Everyone is gone (Mom really should have tried harder to wake me up), so I dash around getting breakfast, getting dressed, and roar into school a few minutes late.

But I do it. I make myself sit still through the last few hours of the last day of grade eight. I never do fully grasp what Civics class is all about, although I can't say I'll miss it.

At least no one could call me a quitter. By now, though, the entire school seems to be in on some weird secret about me. Pretty much everyone is staring at me, or avoiding me, even some of the teachers. Mr. Marcus keeps looking at me sadly in English class. At lunch, Jez tells me that her teacher took her aside and asked if she should be hanging out with me so much.

He wondered if I might be a "bad influence."

I have no idea what Martin told everyone about me, but it can't be good. I sit through the last day of school with everyone glaring at me and avoiding me for some mysterious reason.

I find out soon enough though, after school, when I'm walking C2 and Jez to a celebratory last-day-of-school visit to The Float Boat.

Christine is skipping along the hot sidewalk beside me. She pipes up, "What's a druggie?" Jez and I exchange worried looks.

"What do you mean?" I ask her.

Christopher answers, "Well that's what we heard you are. That and a ..." he hesitates, but only because he can't remember the next words. My quick little sister doesn't have any trouble remembering them, though.

"... an addict," she says proudly, like she just won the spelling bee.

I'm too astonished to say anything. I just stare at her. Jez is quick on the uptake, though, and blurts out, "It means your sister is great at working hard at school. It's an addiction. So she's an addict. Understand?"

Christine nods, but it seems like she doesn't buy it, and eventually she'll have more questions.

Martin told the whole school about me all right — he told them a pack of lies. It turns out he thought it would be funny if he told everyone I was a drug addict. He wasn't even brave enough to tell them the truth about me because it would sound so ... what?

Interesting?

Bizarre?

Honest?

Martin Evells is the worst human on the planet. Part of me is relieved that he's too scared to tell the truth about how he treated me and what happened in the playhouse and after, but the lie hurts. I'll never live it down in this place.

I storm into The Float Boat fighting back tears, and there are so many kids in here, I just know I won't be able to talk to Mrs. Forest. When I do fight my way to the counter and come face-to-face with her, she seems surprised, then really happy.

"Gwen! I've been expecting you," she says. Her face is hot and shiny with sweat. Her arms are busy with the float machine, but she manages to look all-over glad.

It calms me a bit.

"Yeah, I've been wanting to see you, too, but I've kind of been under house arrest," I say, dropping my voice. She nods but doesn't say anything else. There are kids all around us, buzzing like bees.

"I think I might see you later … tonight," I say quietly, but I'm not sure she hears me due to the infernal shouting. She just smiles and says, "That's $3.45 for the lemon drops and the jelly beans."

I pay her, and Jez and the twins and I go back out into the hot afternoon. The store is like a giant beehive of activity, and it gives me an instant headache. The bright afternoon doesn't help, either. I blink and tell Jez I'm going home — my head hurts.

I drag my brother and sister home. A few kids ride their bikes past us and shout things at me like, "Freak!" or "Druggie!" Jez yells at them to shut up, but I keep a stony face. Christine wants to ask more questions (it doesn't take her long), but one look from Jez tells her not to say a word, so she skips obediently ahead of us on the broiling sidewalk.

This is going to be a long summer. The best I can hope for is that people will get back to ignoring me, like usual.

When we get home, the Chrissies race around all excited because school is over, but I just can't join in. They get their bathing suits on, and I turn on the sprinkler for them in the backyard and then sit on the picnic table, watching them squeal and play. I'm a long way away from them, even though I'm sitting right here.

I hate Martin Evells with all my heart. I'm going to be an outcast my whole life because of him. Jez is going away for the summer, and the entire town thinks I'm a drug addict because of a lie. They weren't that keen on me before, but now they actively don't like me, or worse.

The only thing I'm really good at is flying. All I want to do with my life is get out and fly above the troubles of this crappy world.

And keep flying until I figure a few things out.

I decide on one thing: I'm going out flying tonight whether anyone knows or not.

I did tell Mrs. Forest. And it's not like I fully intend *not* to tell anyone else I'm going, but in the heat of the moment I don't.

And I will forever after wish that I did.

THIRTY-SIX

It's late. Mom is sleeping. The twins are sleeping, finally exhausted after their last-day-of-school-sprinkler-party-of-two. I'm leaning against my window, playing with the little lock, pushing the window screen open further and further. Finally I just do it and push the screen all the way open.

The warm breeze actually smacks me in the face, like a little slap. It picks up my hair and dances it up and down, and says, "Come on out, Gwennie." I suck in a huge lungful of air, and it's warm and deep and green and wakes something in me, and before I know it, I'm outside.

And I'm zooming, and soaring, like the first night. There's no worrying about air-walking or air-swimming, or how to control myself, my body is just forcefully aware of its freedom, and I'm gone. In fact, I'm so far gone, I'm not sure I can get back.

Before I realize it, I fly so high that my town is well below my feet, and at first I can still see houses and buildings, and cars that get smaller and smaller.

But then the town becomes a large ball of light below me, then quickly becomes a smaller and smaller ball of light, surrounded by the dark, black world.

Then all my life and all my family memories and Cassie and Jez and anything that keeps me tied to this world at all is just a tiny speck of light below me, and I could be out of the atmosphere for all I know. The moon is so huge and the stars are so bright, and I'm among them. The planet rolls along beneath me, a bright blue ball, and I see us all clinging to it like a baby on a mother's hip.

I feel a sudden warmth then, a goodness about the home so far below me, the place I come from. As I hover and watch the curved Earth as it spins below me, I hear a buzzing in my right ear.

I ignore the buzz for a while, just looking at the world below me, but the buzz keeps growing and growing. It grows to a loud whine, and I look around me, but there is nothing to see except stars and sky. I dismiss it. I hang and look and see the sky and stars and planets, and I know there is a beautiful power to all this that I wish I could write down some day. But I'm not much of a poet, not according to Mr. Marcus, anyway.

But the buzzing is insistent, and it gets louder. I turn my head toward it, kind of like you would to find an annoying mosquito, and then I see it: there out of the darkness and stars comes an enormous black cloud hurtling toward me.

It rolls forward at me like a giant monster, or a huge black snowball, with bits and pieces of caught things sticking out of it. It's making a loud, roaring noise as it gets closer, like a huge wave, or a screaming crowd. Then I see there are creatures in it. I realize that there is a constant roll of hair and teeth and nails and flying fingers and toes as it rolls toward me ... people, I guess ... but nothing really human.

I see this, and I know the death cloud is coming for me.

I've never heard of a death cloud before, but I just know that's what this is. That's what it's called.

My heart kicks up to a loud pounding, and my whole body is screaming to *move it*! The death cloud is almost upon me, and I probably don't need to look at it twice to figure out it's not exactly a good thing.

But I'm stuck. A coldness starts at the tip of my toes and my head, my heart, say goodbye. This cloud is going to roll over me, and that'll be it. No one will know where I went, or why, I'll just be gone.

That's when my body decides to pitch in and save us.

With a speed and agility I wish I'd shown even once in gym class, my dear body only hesitates for a second then starts to torpedo us back toward Earth, zigging and zagging all the way. I think of those baby antelope hot-footing it away from a cheetah, finding the best path to throw off the predator.

Because the death cloud *is* a predator, I can feel it. It wants me to give in, to say goodbye, to give up at this job of living, of being me. I hear a thousand crying voices in my head, and they're all saying one thing: *You CAN'T FLY, GWENNIE ... this is NONSENSE....*

My heart takes on a fierce pounding and I feel that funny tingling and freezing in my arms and legs. *I don't need any fatal plummeting at the moment, thank you!* I yell at myself.

I open my eyes and take a peek around me, and the spot of light below me is growing. My town is growing beneath me. I'm getting closer.

And as soon as I see my town, I feel a tiny tingle of warmth. Just a flutter. And I hear one voice out of the thousands louder and clearer than anything. The voice seems familiar but I can't quite place it....

Your body is doing its best to save you, Gwennie, it says. *Maybe that head of yours could lend a hand?*

So I will myself to think. I take another peek behind, and there is the death cloud, hard on my heels, rolling like thunder toward me. There *are* people in there, screaming and crying or just staring out at me. I get a really hard heart then, and my head clearly thinks, "NO!"

You're NOT going to get me. I'm sorry for your predicament, but no matter how sad I am, or how strange or different from everyone else on this planet, you're not going to get me.

I CAN fly, just watch me.

And while my body does its best to steer us back toward Earth, I try hard to think about all the great reasons to stick around....

... I LOVE watching Cassie roll hard in the dirt right after I wash her....

... I DO want to chase C2 around the yard with the hose after they eat purple popsicles, which don't exactly come out of clothes all that easily....

... I LOVE hanging out in the park with Jez on hot summer nights....

... I WILL hold up my head in school despite horrible Martin Evells....

... NO ONE gets to tell lies about me and get away with it....

...I DO want to talk to my mom about my dad....

As soon as I think about my dad, my body sets up a fiercer buzzing. I can start to see the faint shape of houses and roads and parks below me again. My town is getting closer.

But the death cloud is getting closer, too. It catches my toes, and for a second my feet, then my legs, go stone cold. I hear screaming in my head: *YOU CANNOT FLY, GWENDOLYN GOLDEN!!*

I can feel hands and claws and other things I don't recognize (tentacles?) grabbing at something deep inside me. I feel such a sudden sadness that tears are all over my face, and I know that there are scared children in that cloud, and lost teenagers, and mothers and fathers who failed at being parents, and old people who just gave up and quit with the business of living long before their time.

I also know that no matter what, that WILL NEVER BE ME.

And I'm sorry and sad for everyone in that cloud, but I say "No!" again, really loud this time, and my body sheer rockets into town. It's my space now, I'm on home turf, and my body dodges through church spires and school playground equipment, and around the flagpole at the centre of town. The death cloud is hard after me, and I have to keep going faster and faster toward my house. As I get closer and closer to home, though, I can feel my body tiring, and I'm almost finished.

The death cloud touches me again, and I start to hear the voices of everyone inside, and I can hear them crying and calling: *YOU CANNOT FLY!*

I block them out. I have to make it home. My body gives a final gigantic push, and I fly into my backyard, but that's where the death cloud catches me and throws me onto the ground, swooshing over me and settling upon me.

A thousand, thousand sad souls start scrabbling at mine and want me to go with them.

I open my mouth to scream, but nothing comes out. I'm a goner.

Until someone screams louder than I ever could, "Go off, you foul thing! McGovern Everett McGillies the Third says she is not yours to take!"

For one astonishing moment, I see Mr. McGillies at my feet, armed with what looks like a white-hot sword. I quickly realize it's an empty pop bottle glinting in the moonlight and he is brandishing it above his head, but for a moment the death cloud turns from me toward him.

I don't waste any time; I zoom off the ground and up into my bedroom window.

"Shut the window, missy!" I hear Mr. McGillies scream.

I shoot in through the window, and believe me, he doesn't have to tell me twice. I slam that window closed behind me like it's the gates to hell.

THIRTY-SEVEN

When I turn around, my mother is sitting on my bed. For a moment we exchange astonished glances, then she jumps up and hugs me.

"Are you okay?" she says into my hair, and suddenly I'm sobbing and really scared. I start shaking.

My mom makes me sit with her on the bed, and it all spills out of me, how I went too high, how I almost didn't make it back, and about the death cloud. I tell her about what it felt like when it grabbed me, and about the voices, and the rolling black cloud of teeth and hair and fingertips all caught together in a moving ball of blackness and despair.

She seems suitably horrified. I lie down on my bed with my face turned to the wall. I'm still crying. My mom sits on the chair near my desk, fiddling with my pencil case, like she has something to say that she's not really happy about.

Eventually one of us is going to have to speak, so my mom finally spits it out and says, "Gwen, I hate to have to remind you that I told you never to fly alone. It's not safe for you. For Night Flyers. Now you know why."

"Did you know about it? The death cloud?" I ask, my voice muffled against the wall.

"Not exactly. I didn't know it was a thing like that, but your father did tell me there were dangers, especially if you go too high. I should have told you that."

"It told me to give up. It said I couldn't fly," I say.

"Well, I guess it's wrong, and you can," my mother says quietly.

"I had a lot of help from Mr. McGillies. Why didn't the cloud get him, too?"

"Maybe he's got nothing to lose, Gwennie. Nothing that the cloud can take away."

That's a sensible thought. I think about my useless three-page brochure and the annoyingly short answer to question three, about if Night Flying is dangerous.

Generally no, talk to your Mentor for further instruction, really doesn't cut it as an answer, particularly when there *are* some serious dangers out to kill you. The More-than-Willing probably get a whole chapter in the handbook about the death cloud and therefore get to live long, safe lives.

I think about Mrs. Forest and how many questions I have for her. I think about how Mr. Forest tried to help me by answering some of them, like about if there are other flyers. I hear him saying, "There was another one, but he's gone now."

And something clicks inside me, and I make a whole bunch of things come together at once. I have a clear knowing of something, and my brain shouts it out.

"It happened to Dad, the night he vanished, didn't it? The death cloud took him in the storm, that's why we never found his body?"

My mom starts to cry, and whispers, "We don't know, we just don't know," and I almost wish the death cloud *had* grabbed me. Then at least I could be done with this world of pain.

And, presumably, meet up with my dad again.

THIRTY-EIGHT

I spend the rest of the night lying on my bed, facing the wall. Mom sits on the bed for a while, then she has to go to sleep, too. The twins will be up early, and so will she.

Before she goes, though, I turn away from the wall. I stopped crying a while ago, but I have that salty, tight, dried-tears feeling on my face.

"Mom," I say, "when were you going to tell me the truth? About Dad? About how he died?"

She looks at me and I can see she's welling up again. "I'm sorry, I really am. I should have told you right from the start. But how do you tell a child her father can fly? Or that he died possibly because he flew into a terrifying death cloud during a storm?"

I mull that over. I'm not sure, I'm really not. After he disappeared, what bothered me most was that his body was lost. Where did it go? Maybe he was still out there somewhere. I used to imagine him swirling around in deep water where no one would ever find him, or caught in an eternal windstorm, up in the sky, like Dorothy in *The Wizard of Oz*.

Which maybe wasn't so far from the truth.

I needed so badly to know where his body went, that for a long time I wanted my mom to lie to me about it. Really, would a little lie have hurt so much? He drowned. He burned to nothing. He was swept up in an unspeakable horror called the death cloud.

Death by something nasty, whichever way you looked at it. But death by *something*, at least.

"I hoped that flying was something I could just put away forever. I didn't expect to ever think about it again," she was saying.

"The truth would have been better, Mom," I say, interrupting her. It would have been, I suddenly know it now. Somehow I would have accepted that my dad was a Night Flyer, and that he died flying. It would have helped me know him better, myself better, right from the start.

My mom looks at me a long time and smiles a little. She pushes some hair out of my eyes. She speaks after a bit.

"You look so much like him, Gwen," is all she says.

I feel a whole world of deep sadness, and that sad well in me suddenly finds my dad's voice, telling me and Mrs. Forest that I don't like floats. I'm about four and ashamed that I just threw one up on the counter of The Float Boat.

At the same time I remember this, I make another amazing discovery.

"Mom, I think Dad spoke to me from the death cloud. It's what helped me get away." My mom sits up and looks part amazed, part sad.

"He what?" she whispers.

"He spoke to me, and I heard him. He said something like, 'Your body is doing everything it can to save you, Gwennie, maybe your stupid head could help out, too.' So I decided right then and there that I wasn't going to die. It's how I got away."

My mom nods and nods, and gentle fat tears start down her cheeks again. "He would save you, Gwennie," is all she says.

We sit together in the dark for a while. My mom stops crying and we talk a little about Dad, for the first time in ages. We're companions in how much we both miss him, and it's good to share that missing finally, after so long not talking about it.

Now I know that he was a Night Flyer, there's a whole load of stories she can share that I never heard before. She tells me that he and Mrs. Forest were friends and flew together. She says that he put the brass hook on the screen, and he flew out my window almost every night when I was little. It's at the back of the house, and the best window for flying.

She tells me that because she wasn't a flyer, they never suspected that their children would fly. The other Night Flyers all had *two* parents who flew, never just one.

Until now.

It's really late, then Mom finally yawns and says she has to go to bed, but before she goes I ask her one last thing that's been bugging me.

"Mom, what about C2? I mean, Christine and Christopher," I correct myself. "Shouldn't we tell them the truth about Dad?"

My mom sighs and looks suddenly really old. She shakes her head. "If you can think of a way to explain, Gwen, be my guest. Otherwise, we'll have to keep it between you and me for a few years more."

"What if one of them starts flying around? Wouldn't we tell them then?"

She looks worried for a minute, like the thought of the twins with the added ability to fly was just about too much for her.

Then I start to laugh. That would be a sight, my brother and sister zipping around above our heads, all day and all night. No one would *ever* get any sleep, and the town would never be the same. The twins wouldn't care if anyone knew they could fly. People would likely come from everywhere to take pictures of them, if they could spot them flitting around the school flagpole or wherever they chose to raise havoc.

Good luck getting *them* to come in when they're told!

At first I think my mother is going to cry. Then, to my relief, she starts to laugh. And before I know it, we are both laughing so hard that we are actually clinging onto each other, gasping for air.

Sort of like two drowning sailors who sight a lifeboat at last.

THIRTY-NINE

After my brush with death, I spend the next week sticking pretty close to home. One thing I know for certain: I'm not flying again.

Not now. Not soon. Maybe not ever.

I avoid Mrs. Forest, although she does come calling a few times (I just don't answer the door, which is rude rude rude, I know). She also leaves me a note asking me to visit her at The Float Boat, which I don't answer. Also rude.

She stops trying to contact me after a bit. I avoid The Float Boat, and somehow we don't run into each other.

School's out. The Chrissies are in day camp every day — my mom caught on to those pretty quickly, when the twins were about four years old — and they are off doing zoo trips or pony rides, or park hikes from eight a.m. to four p.m., all summer long. It's for the best, really.

They come home each night a little more sunburnt and totally exhausted, which is perfect for

Mom and me.

At the start of summer holidays, I have no plans, except I have one thing I have to do. I have to find Mr. McGillies and thank him for saving my life. I look for him for a while without any luck, then a few days after school ends I do find him rattling along the sidewalk in the blistering heat. It's too hot for normal people to be out, but he's out pushing his cart and wearing his long filthy coat.

I hear him, then see him coming and I stand on the hot sidewalk in front of him, and I say, "Thank you, Mr. McGillies. You saved me from the death cloud."

He blinks at me and brushes by me without so much as a nod. "Mr. McGillies," I say again, "I just want to thank you for saving my life," but louder this time.

He stops and stares at me, then waves his hand. "Darkness doesn't like bottle shine. You ought not to go out alone, missy," is all he says.

That seems almost like a "you're welcome," or the best I'm going to get. At least I said what I had to say. It seems to me that Mr. McGillies is there, saving me from the police or the darkness or what have you, an awful lot. Watching faithfully. A kind word was the least I could do.

After that, I'm free to do pretty much whatever I want. I hang out with Jez. We go to the town pool, or out into the hills for long hikes. I do my paper route on Saturdays. Other kids avoid me, but no one yells anything, not that I hear anyway. A few times I go to play tennis with Jez at the local tennis courts.

Then Jez leaves for the summer, and I'm at a loss what to do with myself.

For a few days I just sit around the house in a sulk while Mom is at work. And then it happens. For no particular reason, I finally start to read.

I don't want to go into this too much, but if I'm totally honest here, the whole Less-than-Willing Reader title has bothered me. It's true, though. I've just never given books enough time.

I choose to change that.

So, not one to set myself a small challenge, I choose to start the summer off by reading all those big books that everyone else has read, about the boy wizard. I've never read them, or seen the movies, which sets me apart. And I'm tired of being so different from everyone else my age in town.

So I go to the library, check out the first boy wizard book, and take it back to the hammock in the backyard. It's well-read, this book. Probably every kid in town has read this copy, it's so dog-eared and the paper is soft from so many thumbs and fingers.

I take a deep breathe, open the cover …

… and I read the whole book in one afternoon.

At dinnertime I'm amazed that it held my attention so easily, and I finished a book more than two hundred pages long. I couldn't put it down.

I was More-than-Willing, which shocks me a little. What, honestly, was holding me back?

After that, it's kind of like watching sharks in a feeding frenzy. I pretty much tear through all those books about the boy wizard and the bad guys (who fly around without a broom, which I think is blatant flight-prejudice, but I let it go). The librarian, Mrs. Danderson, and I become friends. She's known me since I was little, and I've never taken out a fiction book in my life, just books for projects and homework.

She could have said, "It's about time you started reading, Gwendolyn Golden," but she never does. Every time I walk into the library, she's there with the next book in the series waiting under the counter, which she picked off the shelf and saved for me.

My mom doesn't say anything either when she creeps up on me reading in the hammock one afternoon. I don't notice her, I'm so involved in the fourth book (my favourite). She just places a drink of lemonade beside my elbow and walks away.

It takes me a few weeks to read the whole series. I am kind of rusty. Then Mrs. Danderson moves me along to more books, older ones that she explains started the "genre," books about dragons and elves and little men-boys called Hobbits. There's something comforting in reading a load of books about worlds and people that don't really exist, and yet seem so real.

It makes my flying seem downright simple and understandable. I'm not a wizard or a dragon-rider or a fairy queen or anything. Those people are clearly way out there in the land of fiction, and not at all real.

By comparison, I'm just a little out there.

They all have convincing brushes with death, too, which is comforting. The boy wizard is almost killed about forty times by the (non-broom flying) bad guy who is hell-bent on killing him and everyone else. The little Hobbit creatures have to fight a dragon, then a huge whole world of bad guys, all bent on killing them, too.

I know it's fiction, but I finally understand what Mr. Marcus is always talking about: how the story transforms us, even if it's not real. That magic and fantasy can take us places, and let us feel things, and give us valuable experiences, too.

So I spend the first month of summer reading and reading and reading, and I make a choice.

If that tiny Hobbit creature could stare down a dragon, and that boy with the scar could take on the worst kind of evil imaginable, it should be easy for me to do what comes so naturally.

I'm going to fly one more time.

It's time to go and see Mrs. Forest again.

FORTY

The next day is too hot.

It is the very middle of the summer.

It also happens to be my birthday. I officially make it to fourteen years of age today.

It's also the day that I finally drop by The Float Boat to talk to Mrs. Forest again after so long. But when I get there, the store has the big red CLOSED sign on the window. That sign filled me with despair when I was little. Today is no different.

I can't talk to Mrs. Forest today, clearly, since she's not here.

My mom wants me to invite Mr. and Mrs. Forest to my birthday "celebration" in our backyard that evening, so I leave them an invitation in the mailbox, anyway. Even though I've been so rude to Mrs. Forest and ignored her for a month and a half, I know she'll turn up if she can. She's my Mentor.

Which leaves me feeling awkward.

My fourteenth birthday ends up being a strange little affair with just the Chrissies and my mom and me in our backyard. We're eating barbecued hotdogs and tossing tiny pieces to Cassie when Mr. and Mrs. Forest *do* arrive to liven things up with a huge white frosted cake.

At first I'm shy, but Mrs. Forest doesn't let me stay shy for long. She just hugs me and says hello and doesn't mention how rude and absent I've been. Things are fine between us, just like I'd been in The Float Boat every day, chatting away to my heart's content.

There's an angel, a golden candy angel with wings, on the top of the cake.

Cute.

The Forests closed The Float Boat today to buy me this golden candy angel from a bigger candy store in a bigger town down the highway.

It makes me feel like I'm about eight years old, but the cake is really tasty and it's nice of them to think to bring it. The golden angel on the top is made of something called "marzipan," which tastes all wrong to me, sort of like perfume and salt, but I munch a tiny piece obligingly. Luckily the Chrissies love it and finish it off, fast. I try not to be disturbed by the sight of a golden angel wing dangling from my brother's cake-covered lips, like a cat devouring a butterfly, wings last.

I'm opening a gift from C2 (it's a giant water gun, so I can *really* get the purple popsicles rinsed off them) when Mr. and Mrs. Forest have to leave.

Before she goes, Mrs. Forest tells me to come to the store later, that she has something to tell me. She smiles at my mom, who smiles back.

I'm intrigued. I decide that now all is forgiven, I will go and chat with her. I feel a tiny bit excited by this, but I really have no way of knowing, not right then, just how exciting things are about to get.

After I help my mom clean up the dishes and food from my birthday dinner, I head out with Cassie. I wear the swishy green shirt Mom gave me the night of Martin's party, just to remind myself that it's a birthday gift, too. Mom managed to get out the soda stain and fix the missing button. Cassie and I walk along the quiet streets in the warm night air. It's really a beautiful summer night.

I'm at the open door of The Float Boat when I notice Mr. and Mrs. Forest rocking gently on the porch swing together.

"Well, Miss Golden, are you ready for another party?" Mrs. Forest says as she hoists herself to her feet. I swear there is excitement in her voice that perks up my ears and makes my heart swell, just a little.

Party? What is she talking about? I follow her inside the store, into the cool, dark, candied air.

"This came for us today." She reaches under the counter and hands me an envelope. It's a creamy, expensive-looking yellow envelope with "E.F. & G.G." written on it.

"We're invited to the Midsummer Party," she says. I open the envelope and take out a feather stamped out of gold tissue paper. It's the same shape and size as the golden feather in my handbook. There's nothing else in the envelope but the feather.

"What's this?" I ask, eyeing it.

"It's our invitation. It came today. I'm picking you up at your bedroom window, tonight at 12:01 sharp. Wear something white. Bring your feather."

I am about to protest and say I need to ask my mom, but she tut-tuts and says, "Don't say anything about your mama, girl, she knows where you're going tonight. I already told her." Mrs. Forest bustles away into the back of the candy store, and she says over her departing shoulder, "You be ready at 12:01!"

Then she chuckles.

I shrug and am about to head outside again into the evening when I hear a little laugh and realize Mr. Forest is standing over by the jelly beans. He must have followed us inside and is now slowly filling up jelly bean jars, one by one, from big bags. Funny, I never thought about the jars being empty enough to be refilled. They are always full. It occurs to me that many things must happen in this world, keeping it steady and working along, when we aren't paying attention.

"There's no arguing, Gwen. It's midsummer tonight, you know. You might as well just give in and enjoy it."

I'm a little worried. This is my first time flying in a long time, and I'm not sure what Mrs. Forest has planned for me.

"Mr. Forest, am I going to get hurt?" I blurt out.

"No!" he answers, surprised. He puts down the big bag of jelly beans he is holding: licorice whip. He puts his hands on his skinny hips and listens to me. I spill it, fast.

"Well, it's just that I'm wondering if anything in particular is going to try to kill me tonight, like the last time I went flying?" I can see that I'm suddenly a little more nervous about this than I thought. I fiddle with the golden paper feather in my hands.

He looks concerned. "You're talking about the Shade, Gwennie?"

Now I understand that the death cloud has a name. "Yes," I say, not looking at him. I don't want him to see the worry on my face.

"You should be scared of it. Lots of Night Flyers don't come back when they meet up with the Shade. It's amazing that you did. You must have some fight in you, girl."

"How did you know I met up with it?" I ask, ignoring his last comment. I thought the death cloud was my own secret.

"Your mom told Mrs. Forest," he says. I know this is going to make me mad if I think about it, my mom telling Mrs. Forest about that night without my permission, so I don't think about it.

"What is it? The Shade? There are ... people things in there," I say quietly. I start to breathe fast and my heart starts to race. That bad night is coming right back at me.

Mrs. Forest comes out of the back room and rests against the countertop: "They aren't people, Gwen," she says gently. "They're the sad parts we remember, the memories we can't forget. We put them there, in the Shade."

"We do? How do we?" I must sound like a little kid.

"Because we can't let them go. Or we're sad for them. Or they're sad for themselves for one reason or another. Maybe they didn't live right, or they didn't love right, or they didn't do right. The Shade takes all that wrong and makes it into ball of misery, just waiting to find us, any of us, when we're weak, or scared, or lost," Mrs. Forest answers.

I'm not sure I understand.

"Well, why is it especially dangerous for Night Flyers?" I'm still not getting it.

"Because it wants us to quit what we're best at. The Shade wants us all to quit when it finds us. Which means the end for a Night Flyer who has gone too high, if you know what I mean."

I think of how the death cloud found me and chased me, and I nod. I do know what she means. Exactly.

"It takes strength to say no, and escape like you did," Mr. Forest says. He sounds almost proud of me. Suddenly a small part of me feels a little amazed at me, too.

Mrs. Forest holds out her hand. There's a Hershey's Kiss on it. I pluck it from her and unwrap it. Cassie thinks I'm going to give it to her, but I pop it in my mouth, which seems mean, but my dog doesn't need any treats. Really.

"We'll talk more about the Shade, but not now. Not tonight. I'll see you at 12:01 sharp, you just be ready." Mrs. Forest walks away, gone into the back room for good.

"Mr. Forest," I whisper through chocolaty lips. "Mr. Forest, if there *was* anything I needed to know about, anything that might try to hurt me, or kill me, or anything, you'd tell me though, right?" I ask again. Wow, I really *am* worried about flying again.

He walks over and puts a hand on my shoulder.

"Now you listen here, Gwendolyn Golden. You are never going to get hurt with Mrs. Forest around. And you are in for the time of your life tonight, I promise."

He turns back to the jelly beans, and no amount of pestering on my part can turn his attention back to me.

As far as he's concerned, I'm already long gone.

FORTY-ONE

It's 11:59 p.m. My birthday will be over in one minute. There is still a gentle, soft glow in the sky, like the sun is really sad about leaving us behind until tomorrow.

I'm wearing a white cotton blouse and white shorts and white sandals (and if you must know, a white bra and white undies). I'm not exactly sure how much white Mrs. Forest meant when she said wear white, so I pretty much plastered myself in white from top to bottom. Except for the golden feather my hands are fiddling with, I'm white from head to toe.

It ought to be enough white for one person.

My mom is fast asleep in her room. The twins are fast asleep with Cassie downstairs in the living room. It's so hot tonight that Mom took pity on them and let them sleep downstairs on the living room floor, where it's cooler, much cooler, than upstairs in their bedroom.

I'm waiting with the window and screen wide open. I'm waiting for my night to begin. I have absolutely no idea what to expect, though. None of the adults is about to fill me in on anything, which hardly seems fair. I asked my mother earlier what was going on, but she just smiled and said Mrs. Forest asked her not to tell. I found Mr. McGillies and asked him, too, but there was no way to know if he actually heard me, or understood my intent. He just rattled on by with his cart, ignoring me.

And the Micro-Edition for the Less-than-Willing Reader is once again Less-than-Weighty on the subject at hand:

#8: What Ceremonies and Parties do I attend?
As a Night Flyer with full privileges, you may now attend the First Flight Ceremonies of any other Night Flyers in your community. You may also attend the annual Midsummer Party. Ask your Mentor for further information regarding the latter.

I'm wondering if I will ever get my Less-Than-Willing status changed. If the people who decide these things will ever see me as *More*-Than-Willing? Just how do I let them know that I read a lot this summer — two whole series — eleven books in all? And now I'm starting on a whole new series about those blood-sucker vampire teenagers, which is oddly thrilling because they fly, just like me without a broom or anything, and they're the *cool* kids in school. Frighteningly, deathly cool.

I'm fiddling with the hook on the window pouting about this injustice, when suddenly Mrs.

Forest is there, dressed in a long white gown and a flowing white feathery scarf around her neck. Her hair is tied up in a white kerchief, so her dark skin is perfect and glowing and she looks like an angel.

I'm all shy, and don't know what to say. She laughs, offers her hand, and says, "Come on out, Night Flyer Gwendolyn Golden, your night is about to begin." I hesitate, but only a little. I smile and take her hand, and Mrs. Forest and I sail away into the dark, beautiful night, like two white boats on a dark ocean of sky.

We glide silently over the treetops, and soon we're out of town. We fly over the tall cornfields, and I can't help it, I get a little giddy and I want to zoom around. I drop Mrs. Forest's hand, and she says "It's all right, go girl," and that's all I need to hear. I zip around the corn, and through it, and over it and around it. It smells like growing things, and good earth, and sunshine and rain, and I've missed it. It's been calling me, but I put it away until now.

The Shade took it from me for a long time.

We are still making our way somewhere, but playing in the cornfield is fun and Mrs. Forest isn't in any hurry. She lets me play for a while under the whole white moon and the shining sky. But then she says we have to go, and I breeze along the tops of the corn, across the field, letting the silk tassels and topmost leaves brush my belly and fingertips as I fly past. There is a gentle *shushing* and living sound in the tall corn, in the dark earth, in the goodness below me.

We fly a long while, an hour or more. She shows me how to fly on my back if I get too tired flying on my stomach, and it seems a lot like when I learned to float on my stomach, then on my back, in the town pool when I learned to swim. We cross more cornfields and farms with sleeping cows and horses.

There are no people, no cars, no street lights, just a wide open world and the two of us white angels floating over treetops and fields and country roads.

I am burning to ask more about the Shade, and it's awfully hard not to feel a dread about it. But I know it wouldn't be a good thing to talk about right now. I also know, somehow, that Shade or not, I am safe right where I am. Warm breezes are blowing us along, and soon I can see a glow ahead of us.

We are approaching a town.

Mrs. Forest and I glide along the outskirts of town for a while. I know this town. It is two towns away from mine, but it takes a while to drive to it, the roads not being very direct. Flying is faster, straight over the cornfields. Occasionally a farm dog picks up our scent and starts barking, but we keep moving and no one sees us.

Mrs. Forest doesn't take us into town, but sticks to the back roads and lone farmhouses, until we come to the woods. I didn't know these woods existed, but there are the trees, huge and looming and green.

These trees are old. I can tell because I've never seen anything so tall. I fly and look up and Mrs. Forest says, "They're old growth, Gwen. They've been here for as long as anyone can remember. As long as the old stories tell us there have been Night Flyers, there have been trees in this spot. We have always gathered here." They are like the trees on the cover of the Night Flyer brochure, with the smiling girl about my age.

We?

I get a little twist of excitement all through me.

We fly into the woods, me following Mrs. Forest. They are wide trees, much wider than I could put my arms around, wider than four people could put their arms around probably. And they stand tall as any building in a city (although I can't say for sure, since I've never been to the city). They are thickly growing together, but Mrs. Forest seems to know her way, and we wander and twist and zig-zag deeper and deeper into the trees, where it's almost impossible to get through them. Sometime after a few minutes of flying, I start to hear a gentle murmuring and see a faint light up ahead.

We reach what must be the centre of the forest, and there is a clearing, which glows a little. When we break through the trees, I see several people all dressed in white, flying around in lazy circles, like they have been waiting for us.

Some of them fly up to Mrs. Forest and hug her, and I know something important right away. We are among friends, and they are all Night Flyers, just like Mrs. Forest and me.

FORTY-TWO

I look around the great circle ringed by enormous, ancient tree trunks. Best I can describe, a soft light is coming from each of us and our golden feathers. Everyone has a feather, just like mine from the handbook.

There are eleven people, with me twelve. We are every age, floating around in the opening in the trees. Old people, young people, married people, single people, all colours and sizes.

And me.

I feel a little overcome. I'm floating beside a tree at the edge of the group, when Mrs. Forest remembers me and flies over. She takes me by the arm and starts to fly me around the group, introducing me to everyone.

Now, I've never been the most outgoing of people. I find it really hard to mix in with strangers. But for some reason, tonight I don't mind being the centre of attention. I am usually terrible remembering people's names, but on this night I can't forget a thing.

Mrs. Forest first introduces me to Gramelda Insted, an ancient lady with wrinkled lips wearing a funny white frilly gown. She does a perfect curtsy, right there in mid-air, and I somehow curtsy back (didn't know I could curtsy on dry land, let alone in mid-air). She makes me laugh by telling me a strange story about how she once made a pig fly at night (she carried it in her arms while she was dressed in black), so she could scare her older brother through his bedroom window.

I immediately think of Martin Evells and his bedroom window. So I'm not the only one who scares people through their windows. I like her immediately.

Then Mrs. Forest flies me over to meet a young married couple, who introduce themselves as Drew and Dean Evershot. They run a grocery store somewhere in a town I've never heard of, and they seem very nice. A child is floating sleepily nearby, her eyes closed and yawning, a girl who can't be more than about eleven. This is their daughter who has just had her First Flight. They announce this proudly. The child is so sleepy, I wonder what point there was in bringing her, but I keep my opinion to myself.

I meet a teacher named Rajiv, a fireman named Chan who didn't have his First Flight until he was twenty-one (which was quite a surprise, apparently). I meet two sweet, smiling women, Sarah and Sofie, smart and unbreakable, and best friends, too. One by one, Mrs. Forest introduces me around the little group, until we come to the last two people, brothers named Emerson and Everton Miles.

Miles-the-Elder works in a car dealership in the city. Miles-the-Younger is a boy, exactly my age, and exactly the kind of boy I dreamed about, back when I liked boys. Before Martin Evells ruined them for me.

After I meet everyone, Mrs. Forest and Miles-the-Elder fly into the middle of the group, say hello and welcome to this year's Midsummer Party. They say a special welcome to their newest members, Gwendolyn Golden and Diana Evershot. I don't even blush when everyone claps and says my name, which is amazing. Normally I'd hate the attention, but tonight I don't. Mrs. Forest and Miles-the-Elder talk about some other things I don't understand ("Flight Path Agreements" and something else that sounds like "Outer reach sounds of the bore-real-ass" but probably isn't).

Then the business part of the meeting is over, and I can feel everyone is suddenly quiet and expectant. Mrs. Forest tells us all to fly to the top of the nearest tree, which we do. Then we are supposed to drop our golden feathers.

I take my feather from my pocket and gently drop it into the clearing below me. A dozen beautiful fluttering golden feathers fall from the treetops, but they don't hit the ground! Oh no! Instead they hover and dance in mid-air, like shimmering golden birds. They get brighter and brighter until they are almost too bright to look at. Slowly, one by one, the Night Flyers glide down among the floating feathers and start to dance.

I'm the last person to come down from the trees and join in. It's that boy, Everton Miles, who keeps looking up at me and calling me down with a smile. I shake my head, the final holdout, but eventually even I can't resist. The humming is so sweet and the golden feathers are so mesmerizing, and the Night Flyers so happy, holding hands and moving to the gentle sounds, that I finally fly down to join them all.

The humming grows, and we all hold hands and dance and fly and dance some more. I amaze myself and start to hum too, like I know this song. If you've ever been in a choir, where you didn't really pay much attention, you'll know that humming along isn't really all that hard. We do this humming and dancing a long while, and it's the sweetest thing. I hold hands and dance and hum with Gramelda Insted (who is a surprisingly graceful dancer), Chan the firefighter, Mrs. Forest, then everyone. The space in the trees is glowing and golden, and I'm light and happy.

Then they arrive.

The Spirit Flyers.

And I don't know from where, but they come in their astonishing, peculiar beauty. A dozen Spirit Flyers come down from the dark sky, blazing into our midst like a shot of candles or starlight. We mortals are stilled like the trees, with a golden feather suspended in the air before each of us, waiting. I can't say why, but I know to take up a place and float, patient.

Then, one by one, the Spirit Flyers choose. A few Spirits glide by me, and I feel warm and safe, but they don't stop to look at me; they move on and stop in front of another. Then a dazzling white form comes and stops before me. He raises a shining hand and my feather flies softly through the air and tucks behind my ear, a golden hairpiece.

The Spirit is so bright, I can barely stand to look at him. He is a boy. Younger than me and older, much, much older at the same time. He looks at me a long while, and I know that he somehow knows all about my recent brush with death and about Martin Evells and his lies, and about Mom and C2 and about my dad.

He asks me something then, but it takes a moment for me to recognize the words. They aren't so much words as sounds, like a song in my head. My simple brain needs a moment but then manages to decipher what he says, and I hear him say: *You are sad, Gwendolyn Golden?*

I have a sudden thought, like some deep part of me is answering the Spirit: I miss my dad.

Then we are gone. We go to where I can't even tell you. Higher than the night that the Shade found me. We go higher, much higher, much faster. We go through stars and planets and comets, through galaxies maybe, then finally to a humming yellow and white place with stars for a heartbeat. The shining Spirit Flyer and I hang there a long, long time, minutes, hours, days, a lifetime maybe. I'm so warm and comfortable, I never want to leave this place. This place knows who

I am and that I'm from here and I'll be coming back here again, one day.

After a while of being suspended in the warmth and light, the Spirit's voice arrives like a song in my head again, and my poor mortal brain hears his words as best it can. And what he says is this:

Where you think you have enemies, Gwendolyn Golden, you do not.

Suddenly the warm yellow light around us turns into an image, and I see Martin's face looking around, trying to find me in the trees the night I was a crazy person outside his house. He looks worried. Then I see his mother's face, and all she looks is mad. Her lips are saying in slow motion to Officer Scott B. Taunton, "… she's that crazy girl, Gwendolyn Golden. She's … on … drugs."

And a bunch of things suddenly make sense.

Martin isn't my enemy. His mother is the one telling lies to people, about me being on drugs. Her knitting group, her exercise class, the church ladies auxiliary, and anybody else who would listen. It's not hard to whip up a storm of rumours in a little town like ours.

Then something else occurs to me. Martin's mother is probably the one who didn't want us to play together anymore after my dad died, not Martin. Maybe he even missed me, like I missed him.

I'm going to have to talk to Martin. I have to clear a few things up with him as soon as I can. Once I decide that, I feel better about the whole Martin thing, and about myself.

Then the Spirit's voice sounds in my head again. *Where is your father, Gwendolyn Golden?*

"He's dead and gone, Spirit," my voice says immediately.

Another picture appears in the yellow vastness beneath me, and I see my father laughing with me. I'm little. We're playing in the sprinkler in the backyard on a late summer evening, and Cassie is a puppy. Man, she was cute then.

I watch for a long time. There is my little self in a flowered bikini (which Christine still has and refuses to wear or give away), my little puppy, my handsome dad swinging me up in the air, through the sprinkler, again and again. We're both laughing and Cassie is dancing and playing with us in the water. My mom is sitting on the picnic table, laughing too. She looks pregnant, a little swell of twins below her summer dress.

This is what our lives were. We were happy. We loved one another. This is what I have forgotten, what I have very carefully pushed away from my memory, because I just can't afford to remember it. It is too sweet, and gone.

"He's in the dark place, Spirit," my voice says. I can't bring myself to say that he's stuck in the Shade. A tiny spot of worry drains me for a second, but the Spirit smiles and the worry vanishes.

Is he, Gwendolyn? There are many places your father may be, but the Shade does not have to be one of them. You can choose where you keep him. Perhaps when we meet again you will have a different answer for me, and I can show you more.

Choose? A different answer? Show me more what?

My heart beats a little harder. What does he mean? Then the Spirit takes my hand and says very sombrely in my head: *And now you have a different choice to make. You have one year from tonight to decide: will you fly? Or will you stay earthbound forever? There are good reasons to choose either path. It is a difficult choice, and it must be made carefully, Gwendolyn Golden. The next time we meet, you must choose.*

The full gravity of this hits me slowly. *You must choose.* My fifth privilege as a Night Flyer becomes painfully clear. Nothing in this life is easy, apparently, not even the right to embrace our gifts, however offbeat they may be. We must fight and choose our way, right from the beginning.

And I'm sad. I know he's right. I will choose, but not now. There is a big choice I have to make about who I am, and what I am. But not right now, please. And he smiles and says *Okay, Gwendolyn Golden, not right now.*

Then I hear the Spirit's voice in my head one more time: *Where are you happiest on Earth, little golden sister?*

Suddenly I have a strong smell of cornfields, then my Spirit Flyer and I are flying over the largest cornfield ever, without end. We are playing tag and I can't stop laughing and laughing, the corn tickling my hands and feet as we shoot by. We roll and spin and cavort through and in and under and around that cornfield forever, it could be. A giant white moon plays light all around us, and the sweet music of crickets and night owls tell me that I'm a child of the earth, now and forever.

We are perfect, flying in that place, at that time, and it could be that I am flying there still, that a small part of me never comes back, until the world is good and done with things, once and for all.

At some point, though, I sense that the sky is getting lighter. Vaguely I see Mrs. Forest and her Spirit Flyer (who is a dazzling young girl) dancing nearby, in their own part of the cornfield. We all come together and for a time just float and dance and glide and shimmy and giggle and laugh like four kindred spirits who've known one another since the very beginning of time.

The Spirits stay with me and Mrs. Forest in the cornfield, laughing and dancing until the dawn finally wakes us, and they are gone.

FORTY-THREE

I wake up in my bed. The sun is blazing right into my eyes. I sit straight up and gasp, and look around. It's just my dumb old bedroom, with my posters and my desk and my dog once again looking like she is going to burst if she doesn't go out to pee.

Where are the Spirit Flyers? How did I end up in my bed? What happened to Mrs. Forest and the white circle and the golden feathers?

My hand shoots to my ear, but my golden feather headpiece is gone.

I jump out of bed and look out onto the backyard. There is nothing there. No signs of anything spectacular, anyway. A kiddie pool, a picnic table, a sprinkler.

My dad and I played in that sprinkler.

The memory stills me and warms me for a moment. What other memories of my dad lurk in the ordinary objects around this house, I wonder? Suddenly I can't wait to find out.

Just as I am going to pull my room apart looking for my feather, my mom knocks on the door. She comes in with a tray full of breakfast for me. A glass of orange juice, a cut-up apple, a bowl of cereal with milk ...

... and my golden feather tucked beside the bowl of cereal. I grab it and shove it under her nose.

"Where'd you get this?" I demand.

She's a little surprised. "I found it in the backyard this morning, on the ground outside your window."

I nod and grip my feather tightly. It's not a beautiful headpiece anymore, just the feather from the handbook. But it's suddenly more important to me than anything. My mom turns to open the curtains, and I dig under my bed. I open the handbook and place the feather inside, safe.

Mom sits on the bed. "Did you have a good time last night with Mrs. Forest?" she asks.

I nod and start into my cereal. I'm hungry, ravenous, starving like any normal teenager.

"It was that secret ceremony, wasn't it? With the white flyers or something?"

I nod again. I can't tell her about it — I don't have the words.

"I can't tell you about it, Mom," I say through my cereal.

"Not even a little?" she asks. I can hear longing in her voice.

I think about that. "It's not a secret exactly, but it's just too hard to explain. It wouldn't make sense." But she looks so crestfallen and woeful, I have to do better than that.

"Okay, I'll try."

I think hard about what to say and look up at the ceiling for inspiration. It takes a while to come to me, but what I finally say is this: "Well, it's sort of like we're all on this big ball, spinning off in our own direction most of the time. But sometimes for a little, and probably not at all when or how we're expecting, we can meet up and just be happy and spin together. I guess."

I shrug. We look at one other, but I can't think what else to say. I'm a bit embarrassed that something so grown-up-sounding came out of my mouth. Mr. Marcus would be proud. I'm not even entirely sure I understand what I just said.

But my mom seems to. She nods a bit, then gets up and leaves the room.

She comes back in with a box. Dad's box of mementos.

But it's not a box, exactly. It's a book, with all the pages missing to make a box inside. It's a copy of *Your First Flight: A Night Flyer's Handbook*, just like mine.

"It was your dad's book for flyers. He had it when he was a teenager and kept it his whole life. Do you want to look at his stuff with me?"

The morning sun is shining on my mom's hair, and she looks a little like she's glowing. I must be all about spirits today. I still feel like I'm flying around the cornfield.

"Yeah, let's look at it together," I say as I start to eat my apple slices. The twins aren't around this morning. Mom sent them off to a neighbour's house to play. Maybe she was carving out a little time for us. For Dad.

We sit together and she opens the book. It has the same cover as mine, with the happy flying family from the 1950s on the cover. You'd think that the Spirit Flyers might want to update it once in a while. We peek inside ...

... and I get hit with a photograph of a smiling face that looks just like me. It's my dad, about my age, and he looks really happy. I take a closer look and see he's clutching something tight in his hand.

A golden feather.

"His parents took this picture of him after his First Flight ... he's about your age," my mom is saying, but I'm not answering. I pick up that photo and look at my fourteen-year-old father as close as I can.

He had a community, a wife, three children. He was also a Night Flyer, and my father.

There are more photographs in that box, dozens of them. There are some of my dad in his teenage years, doing the yard work, going on holidays with my grandparents, as a young man proud beside his first car. My mom and I spend pretty much the entire morning looking at the photos, talking about them, putting them carefully back in the box, one by one.

And why haven't I ever seen any of these photographs of my father before?

Because he is flying, swooping, and floating around off the ground, happy as a skylark, in every single one.

FORTY-FOUR

At the very bottom of all those photos of my dad flying around and having fun are two more surprises waiting for my mother and me.

The first surprise is a very tattered copy of a three-page brochure: *Your Life as a Night Flyer Starts Today: Your 10 Most Pressing Questions Answered (Micro-Edition for the Less-than-Willing Reader)*.

This is so funny that I just smile and smile, like an idiot.

Something else I learned today: my dad wasn't much of a reader, either.

The second surprise is a golden feather. It's just like my own feather, safe in the handbook under my bed. My mother gently picks it up from the bottom of Dad's box.

"You should have this," she says, then puts it into my hand. She reaches around her head and undoes the clasp of her golden necklace, a gift to her from Dad.

"You should have this, too," she adds, placing Dad's feather on a little hook, then onto the necklace.

I lift my hair and she does the golden necklace up around my neck.

It feels good, this feather and chain. I smile and hug her and follow her into her room to watch her put Dad's handbook away, back in her closet. We don't say much after that, but things are different now.

It's an important day for us, the start of something new.

Before I go out into the hot day my mom does one more thing: she takes my picture. I hold my feather and my dad's feather, and she makes me sit (I actually hover a little) on the picnic table in the backyard.

This photo is going into my handbook, for sure. It's the start of a bunch of pictures I'm going to put in there, and I intend to fly, swoop, and float in every single one.

After that, I go and sit in the park that Jez and I like. I sit in the heat and swing my feet in the dust. I wish I could talk to her, because the Spirit Flyer is right.

I must choose.

Jez is coming back from her family cottage in a few days. School starts in a few weeks. We'll be in grade nine. The entire school hates me and thinks I'm a drug addict. Shelley Norman is going to bully me and will actively try to flatten me whenever she gets the chance.

It's also entirely possible that when school starts, Martin will tell everyone that I'm a monster freak who can fly around at night. But when I think about Martin, I feel a tiny bit better. He doesn't hate me. I know that now. His mom might, but he doesn't.

My hand goes to my chest, and I fiddle with my dad's golden feather. I swirl around on the swing a little.

So things aren't great on the school and town front.

On the plus side, Jez will always be my friend no matter what. And my brother and sister and my mom love me. My dog has lots of good dog years left in her, too. Mrs. Forest will always be my Mentor, and Mr. McGillies, such as he is, seems able to Watch Faithfully.

I lived through the Shade, and I have a Spirit Flyer who shows me the truth. And now I know beyond a shadow of a doubt that my dad loved me, too.

I will choose.

I can stop flying for good. It might be easier that way. No Shade to worry about. Maybe I can convince people that I'm not a drug addict.

Or I can be Gwendolyn Golden, Night Flyer, with my strange gift. And not let the lies bother me.

I hold my dad's feather on my mother's chain, and look up into the late afternoon sky.

I have one year to make my choice. It's going to be interesting, and it won't be that hard to decide.